# Crofton's Fire

# Crofton's Fire

### KEITH COPLIN

G. P. PUTNAM'S SONS

*New York*

This is a work of fiction. Names, characters, places, and incidents either are the product of the author's imagination or are used fictitiously, and any resemblance to actual persons, living or dead, business establishments, events, or locales is entirely coincidental.

G. P. Putnam's Sons
*Publishers Since 1838*
a member of
Penguin Group (USA) Inc.
375 Hudson Street
New York, NY 10014

Library of Congress Cataloging-in-Publication Data

Coplin, Keith.
Crofton's fire / Keith Coplin.
p. cm.
ISBN 0-399-15112-5
1. United States—History, Military—19th century—
Fiction.   2. Little Bighorn, Battle of the, Mont., 1876—
Fiction.   3. United States, Army—Officers—Fiction.
4. Americans—Foreign countries—Fiction.   5. Africa,
East—Fiction.   6. Soldiers—Fiction.   7. Kansas—Fiction.
8. Cuba—Fiction.   I. Title.
PS3603 O682725C45      2004                    2003041407
813'.54—dc21

Printed in the United States of America
1   3   5   7   9   10   8   6   4   2

This book is printed on acid-free paper. ∞

BOOK DESIGN BY AMANDA DEWEY

*For James, Jessica,*
*and Matthew*

Labour to keep alive in your breast
that little spark of celestial fire,
called conscience.

GEORGE WASHINGTON

# One

## I.

SOMETHING HAD GONE terribly wrong.

"Where is Custer?"

"He went down to raid the village."

"Oh, Christ."

The major knew, as I did, that it wasn't a village. It was a city. There must have been three or four thousand Indians down there. And Custer was attacking with less than three hundred men.

"What should we do?" I asked.

The major, a bony man without a lot of sentiment, just looked up at the rise, on the other side of which all kinds of things were happening, and didn't say a word.

Behind us, there were twenty troopers with very worried looks on their faces.

Actually, we were a support group, not attached to Custer's troop. We'd been ordered to find a trail for the supply wagons.

And it was a beautiful day. What irony. The sky a blue that made your eyes ache, not too hot, sunlight as bright as gold, as it could only be out in the West like this. I'm from Rhode Island, and we never get light like this. Or blue in the sky, either. I was sitting on my horse, looking at the blue of the sky, the green of the trees along the river, the yellow-green of the prairie grass. The world's natural beauty, and just beyond the rise, Custer was about to be killed in a horrible fashion.

"Should we help him?" I asked the major.

"No."

"He won't have a chance," I said. "None of them will."

"The damned fool," said the major. "The goddamned fool."

Well, I thought to myself, he was right about that. I'd always thought Custer a fool.

It was odd, but at that moment of great tribulation, I thought of Lucinda, teary-eyed and lovely, with porcelain skin and eyes as blue as the western sky, and her hair, yes, her most striking feature, coal black. Not often did one see such a combination of color in a woman, the alabaster white of her skin, the deep, almost translucent blue of her eyes, and that dark, dark hair. She was of English origin, or so her mother proclaimed, not the *Mayflower* English, but close.

Lucinda was my fiancée, back there in civilized Rhode Island, Providence, actually. She lived with her family on Sycamore Street. Her father was a banker, and a lovely man, much taken with me, I should say (though he wasn't so taken with my profession).

I am Army, with a capital *A*. A graduate of West Point (class of 1874), and I had chosen the cavalry—for the glamour? But mostly for the West. I learned, in my first eighteen months, that there was little, no, let me amend that, no glamour in the occupation of horse soldier. But ah, there was the West.

To a young man of twenty-five, in the best shape of his life, it was pure adventure, and certainly more exciting than my years at the Point, where I had been, at best, only near the best. I'd finished twelfth in a class of eighty-nine.

But for a Rhode Island boy, anything west of the Mississippi River was a new and beautiful world.

"Lieutenant Crofton." The major summoned me.

"Sir?"

"Lead the men back to that group of trees there. We will regroup."

"Yes sir."

And twenty 7th Cavalry troopers could not have been more relieved when they heard the order. Their fallback was made in great haste.

In the trees, partially hidden from any aborigine eyes, we dismounted, holding the reins of our horses, alert to the sounds far distant, sounds of gunfire and men yelling, but drifting, to and fro, with the wind.

Sergeant McCallum asked me, "Are we going to go help?"

I looked at the sergeant, a grizzled older man, a veteran of the War of the Rebellion and a fine and aspiring drunkard.

"Why, Sergeant, do you think we should?"

"Not for Betsy's bells," he said.

We all disliked Custer, a braggart, a malefactor, a hound for glory. But, oh, the man cut a figure on horseback. Back at Fort Riley the children used to run to see Armstrong mount. With his flowing hair and his irrefutable *savoir faire,* he was always a sight to behold.

But he didn't care much for his troopers.

And he cared even less for Indians. "Painted niggers," he called them, or worse. Killing them was sport.

"Crazy Horse is down there," McCallum said.

McCallum might have hated Custer, but he feared Crazy Horse.

"Did I tell you, Sergeant, that I am engaged to be married?"

"If Crazy Horse and his heathens don't cut your throat."

"Why, Sergeant, surely you will protect me."

Not for Betsy's bells, I heard, though he didn't say it.

"Her name is Lucinda," I said, "and she is the most beautiful woman in Providence, Rhode Island."

And there I was, thinking of Lucinda again. Of her warm, dainty hands and her trim little ankles. Oh, God, what she must look like under all those petticoats. We had been engaged a year, but in truth in that time we'd spent no more than two, maybe three weeks all told, together. Yet I had known her all my life. We grew up together, attended school together, were members of the same church, and had written regularly during my four years at West Point.

"It is our destiny to marry," I had told her, a year ago.

"Pshaw," she had responded. "We will marry because you are the handsomest man in Rhode Island, and I am the smartest woman you will ever know."

"And you will be a soldier's wife?"

"For as long as you are a soldier," she had said.

And I knew precisely then that she had other plans for me, a willful and ambitious woman, my Lucinda, with dainty warm hands and trim little ankles.

"Lieutenant Crofton."

"Sir?"

"Take one man and circumnavigate that hill. See what the bloody hell is going on over there."

The major hadn't dismounted like the rest of us. He sat his spotted roan in the dappled shade.

"Sir," I said. Then, back with the men: "McCallum. Mount up."

But he didn't move.

I mounted my horse.

"McCallum?"

Still he didn't move.

"Poor Betsy," I said, grinning. "And she has such beautiful bells."

I spurred my horse, and off I went.

Riding with the wind, my steed in a brilliant ears-back forward plunge, that heavy, rocking motion, the jangle of sword and gun, hat pulled down, leaning forward into the motion, my God, I had never felt so alive, especially when the bullet whizzed by my head with a peculiar slapping sound.

And then I saw them, four natives, one with a rifle, aiming again, off to my left. I swerved, pulling hard on the rein, as the next bullet passed where I would have been, and in a looping, smooth movement, I was around, facing the four charging Indians, going again at full tilt, straight toward them, the reins in my left hand, my pistol in my right.

We closed very quickly, and I killed the man with the rifle. I shot him but three horse lengths between us, dead in the chest, and he pitched back, arms high, the rifle flying.

They hadn't expected me to charge them, and the

other three, thinking perhaps that I had a troop following, wheeled and headed back for the safety of the ridge over which they had ridden.

I didn't follow, but turned back to my right, and right again, to circle the hill, beyond which I could hear a fusillade of fire.

I reached the crest of the long spiny ridge, and down below I saw such carnage that I was sickened. Custer's troop was surrounded by what seemed like hundreds, maybe even thousands, of Indians. The troopers were dismounted, which really didn't mean much, as most of their horses were down. Some used the carcasses for cover. Most just knelt or lay flat on the grass, firing as rapidly as they could.

Custer was in the middle, standing, arrogant to the end, aiming and firing his long-barreled pistol deliberately. And then he was hit. In the back. Then hit again. And I saw it was his own men shooting him. One, two, then a third. They fired their rifles at him. He went to his knees, his head down, and one trooper, a tall, lanky fellow, walked up behind the fallen commander, put his rifle to the back of his head, and fired. Custer pitched forward onto the grass.

I couldn't move from my position. My horse, grown nervous by all the noise, danced this way and that, but I held him, as I held my eyes on the battle below, which wasn't, in any true sense of the word, a battle. Troopers were shooting themselves, or each other. And the Indians were rampaging, leaping in to hack at the dead, tearing limbs from the bodies, gouging out eyes, severing genitals. Even from so far a distance, I could tell that the mutilation would be complete. The savages weren't content with killing alone. Theirs was a rage, merciless and consuming. Like predators, they fell upon their prey, and then they saw me.

One, then another, then, their blood up, a score came rushing up the hill toward me, their horses grabbing at the elevated ground.

Then I felt fear, a fear like none I'd ever felt, a horror so profound and heavy that I almost fell from my horse with it, my heart beating at such an enormous rate that I felt it would fly through my blouse.

My horse must have felt it too, for when I turned and spurred him, he shot forth like a bolt. He lunged so quickly I almost fell off, and the sheer terror of being on the ground, without a mount, had me clinging to the charging animal as one would cling to life itself.

We barely touched the ground. In great leaps the animal sped over the undulating prairie grass, his mane whipping in the wind he made, and I held tightly, one hand with the reins, the other on the saddle horn, my legs clenched so tightly to the animal's side it's a wonder I didn't choke him. I made for the trees, where I hoped to God the troopers still were, never looking back, afraid of what I might see there.

I could hear wild shooting behind me, and a time or two I saw bullets hit the ground in front of me. Thank God they weren't aiming. I was so locked into my fear that the thought of returning fire never occurred to me. All I could think of was the trees, my troop, safety.

And then, in a paralyzing instant, I realized, My God, maybe they aren't there. McCallum. That drunken coward. If he skedaddled, everyone would go with him. And the major, my God, maybe they've shot him already.

And the Indian ponies were gaining. I could hear them now, their hooves pounding the ground, the shouts of their riders clear. Any moment I expected to feel a bullet crashing into my back, or into my mount. I could see, with horrible clarity, the horse falling, and me flying over his head, to hit the ground with a terrible roll, then the savages on me, shooting, stabbing, cutting.

And suddenly there was a crescendo of fire, the airy twang of bullets flying all around me, and behind, yelps of pain, the heavy, lunging grunt of animals. And I could see the troopers, all twenty, standing just at the edge of the trees, firing their rifles, McCallum directing.

Cautiously I looked, and I saw behind me the ground littered with dead, Indians and horses, and those still alive hightailing it back up the hill.

In the trees, I dismounted, my legs trembling, my horse lathered a creamy white.

"Holy Jesus!" McCallum said, taking my horse's rein. "Holy Jesus!"

The major rode up. "What is it," he asked, brusquely, "with Custer?"

"Dead," I said.

"And his troop?"

"Dead."

"Holy Jesus!" McCallum muttered again.

## II.

CUSTER'S DEMISE, and the demise of 261 of his troopers, cast a pall upon the Army. Courts of inquiry were initiated. Newspaper reporters buzzed about. Military careers were threatened. Word of the massacre on the Little Bighorn dampened the Spirit of '76, the Centennial Celebration in Philadelphia and around the country.

As for me, I was questioned. Then I was questioned again, and again. The ghastliness of Custer's end, the waste, bore down on all of us who were there. Sitting in room after room, with intense men seeking answers, I lied. I said I saw nothing, that hostile savages barred my way to the battlefield and that I barely escaped with my life. I told no one of the end of Custer that I had witnessed, his ready killing by his own men. Custer was the fair-haired boy, and I was willing to leave it like that.

Activities against the hostiles ceased, at least for the time being. My troop eventually returned to Fort Riley in Kansas, and there we remained, in garrison duty, while officers from St. Louis and Washington descended on us like clouds from the east. Everyone wanted to know what happened up in Montana on that fateful June day, but no one had yet decided what actually did happen. As for me, I didn't care what had happened. I was just grateful to leave the horror of that day with my scalp still attached to my head.

McCallum, who rightly feared repercussions for his behavior during the battle, was most solicitous of my favor. He treated me with great attention. A drunk and a reprobate, McCallum had, and knew he had, no life outside the army. With all the brass around, he suffered the anxiety of all enlisted men. Officers meant trouble, and gaggles of them meant doom.

Through the remainder of the summer and into the fall, my horse was regularly groomed, I acquired baskets of fruit and a watermelon or two, and once I even found a bottle of fair to middling Kentucky whiskey in my billet. When McCallum saw me on the post, he snapped off crisp salutes that were bladelike in their presentation.

Unbeknownst to the fat sergeant, I had no intention of reporting his battlefield behavior. If I were willing to protect the reputation of a man like Custer, I was certainly going to cast no aspersions on the likes of McCallum. His refusal of a direct order was, after all, merely the reaction of a man in dread and fear, and, if anything, a willful act of common sense. And his directing the fusillade that had neutralized my pursuers erased any rancor I might have held for him. But I also had no intention of easing the sergeant's mind. His worry was a mild source of amusement for me through the hot, often boring, Kansas summer.

And alas, Lucinda. She had read, of course, news of Custer's massacre a week after it happened. The story made all of the eastern newspapers posthaste, and upon my return to Fort Riley, I had a letter.

*My dearest Michael,*

*Oh the worry—I read just today of the horrible happening. My precious one, it is my fervent prayer that you are unharmed.*

*Those awful savages! The scourge of the universe! One can only pray that God will destroy them all!*

*Please please please telegraph me immediately. I must know you are safe.*

*And poor General Custer. My father has said that the man could have been President of the United States. And isn't it pitifully ironic? Such a disastrous end was such a good career move for him.*

*Yours forever,*

*Lucinda*

My parents were equally concerned. I had a letter from them, and a telegram. I was an only child, and though my father understood and was proud of my decision to make the Army my career, my mother had been against it from the start. Father made harness. He was very successful at it, with shops in Providence, Hartford, and Boston. My mother was a writer, one of that damned mob of scribbling women Hawthorne complained of. She wrote romance novels and was successful in her own right. Their concern for my safety was equal to, if not greater than, Lucinda's.

Upon receipt of the letters, I telegraphed both parties that I was safe and well.

And indeed I was, when the interrogations had subsided and life at the post had more or less returned to normal. Among us junior officers, there soon developed a line of humor that crowned Custer the prince of fools. I think all of us had been both contemptuous and envious of the Glorious One. His reputation was, as far as we could tell, far greater than the man. We found him, as a fellow, to be narcissistic and incredibly vain, and as a military man, his grasp of tactics was nonexistent and his concern for the safety of his troopers equally remote. He sat a fine horse. And we were sure that the devil now thought so, too.

"His last words?"

"Where did all these Indians come from?"

At officers' mess, across the rough plank table, four lieutenants and two captains, joshing.

One of the captains, a six-year veteran, said, "It really isn't funny, all those men dead."

"Of course it is, Captain," said the other captain, himself a veteran. "Old Glory Hound treed? The picture of himself that he must have seen."

The first captain smiled. "Had he survived, there would have been a court-martial, I'm sure."

One of the lieutenants, no older than I, said, "He would have braided his hair for that."

And the guffaws, though stifled, measured George Armstrong Custer in the profession.

My major, a lanky Yankee from upstate New York and a career officer, saw no humor in Custer's end. When we had been back at Fort Riley awhile, and when our interrogators had departed, he called me into his office in the fort's administration building.

And there, with just himself and me in the stuffy, hot room, he came of his confession.

"I could not help him. He was beyond help."

The major sat behind his desk, his uniform coat buttoned, even in the heat. His graying hair was plastered against his forehead with sweat. And as I sat across his desk from him, I, too, dressed formally and suffering the heat, I saw his doubt: doubt in his action, doubt in himself.

I said, as slowly and as quietly as I could, "They would have killed all of us. Major, there were a thousand hostiles there. Custer got himself into it. There was nothing any of us could have done."

He looked at me, his pale eyes windows to his despair. "But we should have tried. . . ." He wanted to say more but couldn't.

"And died with him?"

He looked at me, then away, and said, almost in a whisper, "Yes."

"To what end, Major?" I said. "That we, too, could be

martyrs to the nation? Custer was enough for that. The redskins are doomed now. The War Department will turn this into a vendetta. All our sins will be cleansed by blood and fire."

And where I found those words, I do not know. But I knew they were true.

Two weeks later, the major shot himself.

It was a bad end, for he was a good man. He might have put the gun to his head, but it was Custer's ghost who pulled the trigger.

*Dear Lucinda,*

*My Major's suicide was so unnecessary. It is another sin that Custer will have to take into the beyond. What I cannot understand is how the rash and destructive actions of one man can have such devastating consequences. Those of us who served under the Major are at a loss to accept this sad and tragic end.*

*How I long for the comfort of your arms. If I could but lay my head upon your breast, I could lift the cloud from my soul. Life is unjust, my dear Lucinda.*

*Please write me and tell me of your small and permanent joys. Instruct me in your happiness so that I may share it. You are my light in all the darkness.*

*Yours to be and always,*
*Michael*

*Dear Michael,*

*Your last letter touched me deeply. And I am so sorry to hear about your major. But I cannot condone his action. Life is such a precious gift. When someone throws it away, for whatever reason, that is blasphemy.*

*You must promise me, Michael, not to dwell upon this cowardly act. It is a sin against God and a sin against the nation.*

*As for your personal reaction, I find it troubling. As a man, it is your duty to persevere. General Custer was a great man and a great hero, and he gave his all in sacrifice to duty and honor and country.*

*Your major did not.*

*With love and best hope,*

*Lucinda*

My heart belonged, without reservation, to Lucinda. She had been my love and my shield in all my trying times in my service. But her letter put a grained and tinted spot in my thoughts. It did not seem to me that heartlessness could be a part of her nature. Her letter, though, brought such a condition into mind. And I wondered, too, at her assessment of Custer. Was the myth greater than the reality? And could my heart's darling be so naive?

———

Fraternization between officers and enlisted men was not uncommon in western duties, but it wasn't common either. There was in the Army then, and perhaps always, a line between the two groups, and seldom was that line crossed. For one thing, most enlisted men held officers in a kind of benign contempt. And in my experience, this contempt was, all too often, mutual.

An officer could be, and often was, viewed by the men under him as corrupt, overprivileged, and incompetent. Officers often saw those same men under them as lazy, uneducated (which they often were), and dishonest. The Army system, which for the most part followed a European model, encouraged a class system that was essentially unfair. Officers benefited from the system in very fundamental ways. They got better food, better equipment, even better uniforms. And in the cavalry, they had first pick of mounts.

In my years at West Point, I quickly became aware of the elitism afforded the officer class, and added to that elitist scheme was the further elitism of the Point. If as a group Army officers were superior to the enlisted men, West Point educated officers were superior to other officers.

But it was my service with the 7th Cavalry on the plains that I found the real dividing line in the Army. In the open, with an enemy near, soldiers found leaders, and leaders found followers, and rank had nothing to do with it.

"They is not a man who wouldn't skedaddle if he had the chance" was Sergeant McCallum's take on the situation.

"Sergeant," I said, "you are wise beyond your years."

We were drunk, oh my God, as drunk as two men could be. We sat on a rise south of the fort, a full moon turning midnight into day. McCallum had accosted me. There is no other verb to use. Accosted, near the horse barn, where I'd been to see to my mount. It was late evening, after nine, and McCallum had a jug. He was a little bit gone at the time, and brave enough with whiskey to invite me to a parlay.

I joined him. It was purely voluntary. His invitation had touched upon the major. What he proposed, actually, was a wake. We stole away from the fort and climbed the bluffs south of the fort with difficulty. But once at the top, we perched, like two drunken vultures, and passed the jug back and forth.

The whiskey burned like fire.

"It ain't wisdom . . . 'tenant," McCallum muttered. "It's the natural depravity of man." He hoisted the jug and took a mighty swig. "And women, too," he added. "We are a bad lot, every cursed one of us."

"Doomed," I said, as he passed me the jug.

"The major, he was a fine man now. For an officer." McCallum glanced wary-eyed at me. "No offense."

"It's the troubles," I said. "The despair of life. We live with it, but it always consumes us in the end." Then I smiled. "All of us except Custer. Did you ever see him in despair, McCallum? He always had this kind of vacant way about him. And skedaddle? Not Custer. The man had no despair and no fear."

I handed the jug to McCallum. He took it, but before he raised it to drink, he said to me in a low voice, "I'll tell you something, Lieutenant, and it's a deadly thing, a deadly thing."

He took a pull at the jug, handed it back to me.

"Custer?" McCallum said. "He was a lunatic."

I held the jug, looked at McCallum. "You think?"

"As crazy as a three-legged horse."

I drank the whiskey and felt its fire. It was quiet for a while, just the night and the moon, and we two drunken pilgrims.

I raised the jug. "To the major," I said, took a drink, and handed the jug to McCallum.

"The major," he said, and took a drink of his own.

### III.

IN THE FALL, the rains came, turning the grounds of the fort and all about into soggy quagmires. For days at a time, the huge prairie sky was leaden with clouds. There was still no patrol activity, and men grew restless with the rain and the clouds and the close quarters.

It was, then, with a pleasant anticipation that news came of trouble at Lemon Corner, a hamlet about forty miles west of Fort Riley.

"A riot," said the bewhiskered major, a dapper little man with a twinkle in his eyes. He was addressing two lieutenants, Mulvay and Simpson, and me in the deserted officers' mess hall. The major seemed to be having great fun. "Over a whore," he said.

The story did have an element of fun about it. It seems a French whore by the name of Charolais had killed a cowboy, who, as details of the story were revealed, seemed to deserve killing. First, it was reported that he had refused to pay for services rendered, and when the whore insisted on payment, he resorted to fisticuffs. The whore promptly shot him dead.

Justice, particularly of the frontier kind, would seem then to have been served. But the cowboy was from Texas, and the outfit with which he had traveled north was headed by a fiery, unbending type named Eli Walsh. Walsh took exception to one of his drovers being summarily executed by a French whore and demanded justice of a more formal kind.

A sheriff of the county in which Lemon Corner was located was at first cajoled, then flat out threatened, into action. He rode a few dreary miles to Lemon Corner to apply the strong arm of the law upon the delinquent whore, only to be met by armed opposition.

According to the bewhiskered major, "The whore, it seems, had several serious sponsors. And be it for economic reasons or reasons of a lower quality, the sheriff was dispatched by a band of armed Lemon Corner citizens. The sheriff, poor man, was seriously pistol-whipped, and claimed, once he had gratefully reached safety, that he had narrowly escaped with his life."

What happened next could have been predicted. The Texans decided to take the law into their own hands. Some twenty of them descended upon Lemon Corner, intending no doubt to avenge their friend and teach the denizens of this nowhere Kansas town a Texas lesson. But, much to their chagrin, they were greeted by a maelstrom of bullets.

Four of the Texans were shot dead, a half dozen more wounded. Reports of casualties among Charolais's defenders were unavailable. However, by this time it was obvious that the situation had escalated beyond the power of civil authorities, so the Army was called in.

"Lieutenant Crofton," the major announced. "You will lead a troop of thirty men to Lemon Corner and restore order. Lieutenants Mulvay and Simpson, you will take each the same number of troops and seal the roads south and west of the community. Any resistance is to be met with arms."

Thus was I drafted into a whore's war. But like I said, the opportunity to saddle was itself a welcome relief from the confinements of Fort Riley, and I must admit, my men were tickled to go. A whore's war was one of those gifts from the gods, the notion alone worth the trip.

"And what do we do about the French whore?" Mc-Callum asked in the enlisted men's barracks, where I had assembled my thirty troopers and related to them both the background and purpose of our mission.

"We are to arrest her," I said, "and deliver her to the nearest jail for incarceration."

McCallum looked displeased. "That seems a shame," he said.

Most of the other men in the room agreed with him.

"Only did what she had to do."

"It was self-defense."

"They's a law against shooting Texans?"

———

On a bright October morning, a delightful chill in the air and a slight but brisk breeze from the north, nearly a hundred troopers of the 7th Cavalry set out of Fort Riley in a column of two, McCallum and I at the head. There was no brass band to see us off, but there was a crowd, mostly of children who had ducked school to see the proud cavalrymen pass by.

We headed west, over a road that had begun to dry, and it was a grand feeling to be mounted, the jangle of canteens against rifle stocks, the clack of horses' hooves, sergeants down the line barking orders to close up. We might only be going to arrest a whore and her compatriots, but we were the 7th Cavalry, taking with us what glory that august group had accrued.

Our plan was to make thirty-five miles of the forty to Lemon Corner and bivouac for the night. The next morning, Simpson and Mulvay would take their troops to seal roads, and I would reconnoiter the town itself. Once that situation had been properly assessed, I would take my troop into Lemon Corner, declare martial law, and disarm and take into custody any recalcitrant figures determined to be a threat.

The good weather held all through the day, and we made excellent time, arriving at what we considered an appropriate place of encampment an hour before sunset. We did without tents, there seeming to be no chance of rain, hobbled the horses, and soon evening coffee was ready as the supper simmered.

Lieutenants Mulvay and Simpson and I sat at a campfire just at twilight, sipping coffee. Simpson smoked a cheroot.

Mulvay was the first to ask about the whore.

"What if she resists? And you know she will."

"I'll shackle her," I said.

"A shackled French whore," Simpson said. "Now, there's a fancy."

Mulvay asked, "And will you be searching her?"

"I will not," I answered curtly.

Simpson said, "She is a dangerous tart, you know. And she obviously knows how to use firearms."

"I would say," Mulvay said, "a thorough search *after* she's shackled."

"In private," chimed in Simpson. "To preserve her honor."

"Of course," Mulvay said. "But a thorough search, in every nook and cranny."

"Lads," I said, "you've been out here too long."

———

Lemon Corner was not much of a town, two buildings and six tents. McCallum and I lay sprawled in the grass, a bit after dawn, on a ridge overlooking the hamlet. Our horses were tethered at the base of the ridge, and I was studying the community through binoculars.

"A shithole of a town," McCallum said.

"Nobody about," I said. "Here."

I handed the glasses to McCallum. Taking them, he put them up, swung them slowly back and forth.

"I count nine horses, there, on a line behind that north building." McCallum lowered the glasses and spit off into the grass. "That's a saloon, I imagine."

"I wonder how this place got its name," I said.

All the troopers had been up an hour before daylight. Mulvay and Simpson moved their men out just as the sun was edging up in the east. The remaining men drank coffee and cooked their breakfast.

McCallum and I set out to ride the five miles to Lemon Corner, instructing the men in camp to clean their weapons and wait.

It was a beautiful morning, no wind, the light still that clear, edge-of-the-horizon clean. Two roads ran through Lemon Corner, one north-south, the other east-west. They were gray and seemingly dry in the light.

"We go in hard," I said, "and fast. Put guns on everything and hope nobody shoots."

"They ain't got no outriders. I don't see none."

"Give me the glasses."

I looked again, and just west of the north building, I saw a tent with a sign on it. I couldn't read the sign, but I suspected that was Charolais's place of business.

"The whore's tent, there, just west of that north building. I'll bet that's it." I dropped the glasses. "Go fetch the men, Sergeant. I'll meet all of you on the road back there, just below this ridge."

"Aye."

After McCallum had gone, I kept watching the town. In a quarter of an hour, a man emerged from the big building, limped out onto the back porch and relieved himself, then went back inside.

They were all sleeping, I thought. It wasn't yet seven. And if the building was a saloon, as McCallum had suggested, they may have been drinking during the night. Sleeping and hungover, that would suit me just fine.

I couldn't help but wonder why those men down there would fight for a whore. They had killed four Texans. Obviously, they did not intend for the whore to be taken. Or at least, they were not going to abide men coming into their town with violence. But, I reasoned, they were like a lot of men I'd met and seen in the West—shoot first and ask no questions at all. It was a wild place, untamed in every sense of the word. I had heard lethal stories about Wichita and Abilene, when the cattle herds would come north. Dodge City, I had read in a Kansas City newspaper, averaged a homicide a day during the trail endings.

An hour later, the troop arrived. I met them, mounted, on the road east of Lemon Corner. We were below a ridge, so unless some Lemon Corner folk were up on that ridge, they would not have yet known we were there.

I moved the men into a semicircle and talked from the middle.

"We're going to go into the town fast. Have your pistols drawn. But don't shoot unless someone shoots at you first. There are two buildings. I will take the first ten of you and surround and enter the building on the north. Sergeant McCallum will take the next ten and do the same to the building to the south. You last ten men will space yourselves and cover the tents between the buildings.

"Now, we're not here to kill anybody. If you do meet resistance and can use your pistol as a club, do that. Knock the resisters down, but don't shoot them. But, if the situation deteriorates rapidly and gunfire does break out, hightail it back to this ridge and we'll regroup and figure out another strategy. Don't stay in the town and exchange gunfire. You men who come in with me, we will linger and provide cover fire until everyone is out of the town.

"Does anyone have any questions?"

And the men drew their pistols.

## IV.

EVERYTHING WAS a whirl as we descended the ridge into Lemon Corner.

We were charging hard, the column moving with great speed, the horses caught up in the collective excitement, but the men not uttering a sound. There was only the sound of the horses' hooves, a wild and clattering cadence.

At the head of the column, I kept watching as the town drew closer and closer, but still not a man to be seen, the town as quiet as if empty. At the big north building, I directed troopers around the building, and at the front I dismounted with two others. We leaped upon the front porch, and at the big door I turned the handle. It opened with a creak, and I dashed inside, pistol drawn. I could hear the two troopers behind me.

It was dark inside, and I was met with an overwhelming stench. As my eyes adjusted to the darkness, I could make out men lying here and there on the floor. A few of them looked up sleepily, but others didn't move at all.

"I want all you men to lie very still," I said. "And those of you who can, please put your hands up in the air. If you are holding a weapon, you will be shot."

There was no resistance here. I was sure of that. These men were beaten already.

Slowly, I counted, two in front of me, another three to the right, four more at the back, nine. But only two had their hands up. One of them lay only a few feet from me.

"What has happened here?" I asked him.

He was a young man, only a teen. He looked very scared. He had a wispy mustache and long, dirty hair. He was sitting up, hands in the air.

"The Texans," he said. "They kilt some of us."

"Are you wounded?"

"Yes," he said. "All of us are."

There was a ruckus outside. I heard horses. Then I heard someone mounting the porch.

"Lieutenant?"

It was McCallum.

I turned to look at him.

"Dead men," he said. "They's six bodies in that other building." Slowly he looked around the room, at the men lying there. "Don't look like these boys is doing much better."

"The Texans," said the young man in front of me. "They kilt some of us."

It was a sorry situation. All nine of the men in the big building had been shot. A couple were as close to death as you can be and still be alive, and all seven of the others were badly wounded. The young man who had spoken with me was shot in two places, hip and thigh.

We only had one aid man with us, and he didn't have what he would need for so many wounded. But he did set about cleaning wounds and checking with the two dying men.

The youngster related to McCallum and me how the Texans had ridden in, all bold and brassy, and demanded the woman. Big Jim Clancey, the owner of the building we were in, met the Texans out on the porch. He told them the woman had only protected herself, and the Texans best ride on. At which point the leader of the bunch shot Big Jim dead, right there on the porch. And then all hell had broken loose. Gunplay everywhere, men falling, horses bolting.

"Where is the woman?" I asked.

"She be in her tent, over yonder." He nodded with his head.

"All these men were shot, then?" McCallum asked, indicating the men in the room.

"Shot us all. But we kilt some of 'em."

"Yes, you did," McCallum said. "Son, why did you do it? Why did you men fight for the woman?"

He looked at the big sergeant, a fierce look in his clouded eyes. "She's our'n," he said.

I set the men to tending the wounded as best they could, aiding the lone aid man, then I sent two riders to fetch Mulvay and Simpson and their commands. Two more riders were sent to the county seat, the nearest town, to get a doctor and some wagons.

Outside, on the building's front porch, McCallum said, "These boys took a licking, and for what? The whore?"

"She's their'n," I said. "Men fight for women. You know that."

"For women," said the sergeant. "But for a whore?"

Back in Rhode Island, I would have had trouble understanding this situation, and when I was at the Point, too. Within the confines of a well-ordered society, the actions of the men of Lemon Corner would have been inconceivable. But this wasn't a well-ordered society. This was the West. And I'd been out here long enough to know that whatever rules might work in the East didn't work worth a fudge west of Kansas City.

First of all, at this time there simply weren't many women in the West. I'd guess men outnumbered women twenty, fifty, maybe a hundred to one. And what women there were weren't to be found in bugscuffle rat holes like Lemon Corner. They were mostly in towns like Wichita or Denver, cow towns or mining towns. And that our valuable little Charolais was a whore was no surprise. Most of the single women west of the Missouri River were. The only unique aspect of the Lemon Corner donnybrook was the willingness of these men not only to kill to keep Charolais, but to die to keep her.

This approached something sacred, something almost patriotic, and in an absurd way, it was to be admired. The tone of the boy's voice, the menacing look in his cloudy eyes, these features spoke of commitment, the will to sacrifice one's self to a higher cause. Whore or not, the woman at the heart of all this bloodletting was, only in a matter of degree, different from Menelaus's Helen, and the epic slaughter of Lemon Corner was of the kind of Troy, only smaller.

"We have a classical situation here, Sergeant," I said to McCallum, stepping down off the porch. "Only the Greeks could have thought of something like this."

A corporal reported to me that the seven tents between the two buildings were empty except for one.

"That 'un, with the sign. They's someone in it, but we didn't think we ought to do anything about it." The corporal wasn't anxious to take any action at all.

McCallum and I walked toward the signed tent.

## CHAROLAISS EROS EMPORUM

McCallum, cocking his head to look at the sign, said, "What's an eros emporum?"

"It's a fancy cathouse," I said.

"Well," said the sergeant, "I suppose she's in there, taking tea."

I had holstered my pistol, and walked now to the tent's opening, though it was folded shut and I couldn't see in.

"Ma'am?" I said, softly. "I'm Lieutenant Crofton with the Seventh Cavalry. May I talk to you?"

I heard a rustle in the tent, but there was no answer.

"Ma'am, there are a hundred troopers with me. Your

townsfolk have been shot up pretty bad. We've sent for wagons and a doctor."

Still no answer.

I turned to look at McCallum.

He shrugged his shoulders and gave me a couple of wide eyes.

"Ma'am, I'm afraid I will have to insist. I am opening your tent flap now. Don't be afraid."

I gently pushed aside the flap, and there she was, Helen of Lemon Corner.

Why, she's just a child, I thought. A teenaged child.

She sat, at the back of the tent, a blanket around her. It was light enough inside the tent to see that it was tidy, a rug covering the floor, and a picture hanging from the sloped ceiling on the left, a crude drawing of a crescent moon.

The girl (for there was no way she could be judged a woman) had light blond hair, long, but brushed away from her face. And even in the still light, I could see that her eyes were sky blue.

"Are you all right?" I asked, bending, my head just inside.

Her eyes were fixed upon me, and they didn't show fear exactly. In fact, they were quite businesslike.

"Do you speak English?" I asked.

But she only looked at me, didn't make a sound. She didn't even seem to be breathing hard.

*"Parlez-vous anglais?"* I asked.

And then she shot me. I felt the bullet hit my chest, then I felt nothing at all.

## V.

I SEEMED to be in a great and dark river. I was conscious of movement, and every so often I could make out sounds. But I drifted. And I felt very tired. There was no pain, just a heavy, sodden feeling as if I lay under a great weight. And all I wanted to do was sleep.

## VI.

"MICHAEL?"

I heard the voice, from far, far away.

"Michael? It's me, your mother."

I opened my eyes, but quickly shut them because it was too, too bright.

"Michael?"

"Mama?" My voice was a whisper, and it sounded strange to me.

Then I was aware of my hand being held. It was a strange feeling, the warmth of that hand in mine.

"Michael, honey?"

"I can't open my eyes. It's too . . . bright."

"Leave them shut."

"Mama?"

"Yes?"

"Where am I?"

I was, I would learn, in the infirmary at Fort Leavenworth, just north of Kansas City. And my mother was with me. She had come from Rhode Island. I wasn't dead. That was good to learn. Exactly why I wasn't dead, I would also learn, was a mystery. I had a bullet in my chest. No one had figured how to take it out without killing me. The doctor at Fort Leavenworth, a man named Peavey, had simply plugged the hole the bullet had made and waited for me to get better or to die.

"How long have I been here?"

"Three weeks."

"Three weeks?"

Gone. Three weeks of my life had simply disappeared.

"I'm hungry."

"Good."

But I was still tired, and before any food could be brought, I was asleep again.

I had been shot with a .42 caliber derringer. The bullet had struck my breastplate, which apparently slowed it some, then burrowed into the recesses of my chest, where it stayed. It missed my heart, I would learn, by about an inch. I had been unconscious from the time of the wound, for almost forty-eight hours, but on regaining consciousness, I had thrashed about until I was sedated with laudanum. Dr. Peavey told my mother that hasty action by the aid man on the spot had probably saved me from bleeding to death.

I had been transferred by wagon back to Fort Riley, but the medical facilities there were inadequate for my type of wound, so I had been moved again to Fort Leavenworth. A week after that move, my mother joined me. She'd taken the train from Providence to Kansas City, then a buggy to the fort.

She stayed with me, I would learn, twenty-four hours a day, sleeping on a cot next to my bed.

My mother had fed me and given me water while I was asleep, no easy task, so I hadn't starved to death, though I had lost a tremendous amount of weight.

Peavey told my mother that if infection didn't set in, I would probably live, though he didn't really know how. The bullet, aside from resting comfortably in my chest, had apparently done no residual damage. My breathing was ragged but steady, and Peavey could only guess that the bullet touched upon no vital organ.

There was a letter from Lucinda:

*Oh My Dear Michael,*

*How devastated I am to hear of your wound. Your mother told me. Someone at Ft. Riley had telegraphed her. O pray God you are all right.*

*I sometimes hate that you are a soldier. Couldn't you be a craftsman like your father? How I long to*

*have a normal life with you, reading in the parlor in*
*the evening, attending church on Sunday.*
   *My dear sweet one, please do not die.*
   *If you do, I will never forgive you.*
   *Always and always yours,*
   *Lucinda*

But I, her dear sweet one, was alone, with Mother.

"Why didn't she come?" I asked.

"Oh, Michael, it is not an easy trip."

It was a bleak afternoon, the sky through the infirmary window dark and unforgiving, an iron promise of snow. And it was cold outside, even inside. A coal stove at the end of the barrackslike room was all the heat, and it wasn't much attended. Mother sat by my bed. The other beds in the room were empty.

"But she could have," I said.

"It's expensive, too," Mother added.

Each breath was a pain. I shut my eyes. And then I felt myself smile.

"What, dear?" Mother asked.

I opened my eyes again. "The irony," I said. "To survive the Little Bighorn only to be shot by a teenaged French whore."

"Hush, Michael."

I managed, without Mother's knowledge, to get a note off to Lucinda. It was a ragged piece of writing. I scrawled it on a rough sheet of paper brought to me by a medical orderly, then folded it to send. The orderly was a corporal named Jeb, and I gave him a dollar to mail it. In the note, I explained that though Crazy Horse had missed me, Charolais hadn't. And I explained again the irony.

In retrospect, I should not have sent the note. Or at least I should have been more specific. I thought at the time it was a great joke (actually, I still think it was). The trouble was, Lucinda didn't see the humor.

Which was, for a while at least, beside the point, as I began coughing up great globules of blood. My mother, God bless her, didn't panic, but saw that I got immediate attention, though the attention was, at best, slight. Peavey dosed me with some foul-tasting liquids and felt my forehead several times. Even as sick as I was, I could tell he had no idea what to do. But in two days I quit coughing up blood. I was, though, a wasted man afterward, and fever set in. That was what the doctor most dreaded. Fever meant infection, and as far as Peavey was concerned, infection meant death.

All I can remember is being hot, but shivering as if cold. A really high fever simply puts one under, and for the next three days that's where I was, under, totally under.

Only later did I learn of the exquisite job my mother had done.

It was the orderly who told me.

"Snow," Jeb said. "Yep."

He was a gap-toothed boy from Missouri. He wasn't very bright, but he was a good soul.

"She packed you in snow," he said.

"Snow?"

Mother was gone, to the boardinghouse across the road from the fort, for a bath. She would return at supper.

It was three days after my fever had begun, and half a day since it had broken.

"Thet doctor, he give up on you," said the orderly. "Yo mama, she din't."

"Snow?" I said.

"I brung in buckets of it. We made you into a snow-man. Yo lips turned blue. Whooee!"

I could remember the cold, sporadically remember, the wet touch, a whole stream of feeling, and then I was awake. My bed was dry, and I wondered how that was. I had felt, I thought, water, that I was immersed in water.

"Where is my mother?"

"She gone cross the road, gonna take her a bath. She don't sleep, aw, I don' know, long time. You wuz funny-lookin', packed in all that snow. My, my, I thought we freeze ya."

And again, he grinned his great, gap-toothed grin.

God, I thought, shot, drugged, rattled and rolled, and packed in snow. What next, in my twisted new life?

What next?

Dumped.

*Michael,*

*How could you?*

*I am so disappointed. I've cried myself to sleep every night since receiving your horrible letter. That you could consort with such a creature. And only a child. Have you ceased to be a gentleman? Are your animal impulses so strong that you can shame and humiliate me like this?*

*Oh, I am so glad that that horrible creature shot you. I am sure you deserved it.*

*Never now,*

*Lucinda*

"What did you write to her?" Mother asked.

"That I was shot by a teenaged French whore," I said.

Mother sat next to my bed, a bright morning, the sunlight outside on the snow crisp and white.

"You didn't explain the circumstances?"

I didn't look at Mother. "No," I said, "I guess I should have."

"I would say so. You must write her again and explain."

I looked at her. "Why?"

"So as not to lose her."

"I don't want her."

Mother looked at me, her eyes fixed and staring. "Of course you do," she said.

But in fact I didn't. And it came as a surprise to me that I didn't. For a long time, I wanted, had wanted, the thought of her, but not her, no. Not the real, living woman. She was cold. She was distant. She was, I finally and coldly realized myself, humorless.

Thus ended my relationship with Lucinda. I did feel the loss, but not like I imagined I would. All along, she had been an illusion, a dream-memory almost, that had sustained me when I was frightened or tired or disappointed by circumstances; but now, I realized, she had never been a reality.

True, I had never once strayed from her, with any woman at any time. I had always saved myself for her, as any honorable man would. But then, I had never been severely tempted, either. For two years, my life had been mostly horses and men, and what few women I did encounter were either married or disreputable. I had, of course, savored the idea of marriage and Lucinda's arms, for she was a beautiful woman. But strangely, I had never really thought of her in explicit sexual ways. She simply did not give off that kind of aura.

"Ambition," my mother said later in the morning. "Lucinda is a very ambitious woman. I am sure she has big plans for you."

"Such as?"

"Oh, the presidency, no doubt. She once told me that

your army career would be an excellent springboard into politics."

"She told you that?" I asked.

"She is a very intelligent woman."

"Smarter than me."

"In some ways," my mother said.

"I don't want to be president."

## VII.

"I DON'T understand it," Mother said. "The farther west I came, the less of everything there was. How could you possibly like it out here?"

"I don't know," I said. "It's just so . . . real."

"Real?"

We were, as usual, in the infirmary, but now I was sitting up. I was even drinking, a cup of lukewarm tea Jeb the orderly had brought.

"There is little pretense," I said. "Generally, what you see is what there is."

"But everything is so chaotic," Mother said. "The train from St. Louis to Kansas City? The schedule meant nothing at all. When I asked the conductor about it, do you know what he told me?"

"What?"

"'If we get there, we consider that being on time.'"

I smiled. "They often don't get there," I said.

"And you really like it out here?"

"Yes," I said. "I do."

"Among the heathen Indians and young women who shoot you?"

"She didn't mean to shoot me," I said. "She was scared. By the way, what happened to her?"

"I have no idea," said my mother.

Evening came quickly, the winter solstice near. Mother sat reading, and I was propped up on a pillow, breathing all right with just a tinge of pain. I could see out the windows, which faced west, and I watched as the sun went down.

It was a brittle cold evening. The winter's evening light was layered along the western horizon between a long, low line of clouds and the level black horizon. The sun down, it left a collage of light in that thin shelf between heaven and earth, first a burnt orange, deep and intense, fading to pink, then purple, and finally a brilliantly shaded blue that dissolved into gray, and then the light was gone.

I had sat, transfixed with the color and the light, almost in a trance, allowing the evening to happen to me. And as the sky darkened, I looked at my mother.

She, too, was watching the sky. But she turned to look at me, and I could tell, from the small tone of wonder in her eyes, that she had seen, and felt, what I had seen and felt.

I smiled, and so did she.

Three days later, my mother received a letter from Dr. Marguerite Stein, a physician friend of hers who lived in Boston.

"What does it say?" I asked.

It was midmorning, the sky bright outside, wind gusting from the south.

"I wrote her," Mother said. "Two weeks ago. I've known Marguerite for a long time."

"What does her letter say?"

"She had a difficult time becoming a doctor, but she is a strong and smart person. She's my age."

"Mother."

"In my letter to her, I told her everything I knew about your wound."

"And?"

"It's not good," Mother said.

"Read it," I said.

She slipped on her glasses, took a deep breath.

"'Most probably a calcium deposit will form around the bullet. Perhaps such a deposit has already formed, which might explain why the infection hasn't been worse. However, a foreign object inside the body is a dysfunctional situation. Nothing good can come of it, and in this particular case, I would say there is at least a ninety percent chance that something bad will happen, most likely a tear in the lung sac which will result in internal bleeding, which cannot be checked. The bullet should be removed, the sooner the better. But I should also advise that the chance of surviving such an operation is very, very slim.'"

Mother slipped off her glasses and looked at me.

"Kind of puts me between the devil and the deep blue sea, doesn't it," I said.

It's strange, but I haven't written at all about the doctor who, more or less, saved my life. Nor have I felt the need to write about him. He was a gruff, incompetent man, in spite of my being alive (against all odds). I do know he had no military rank. And he was a drinker. He smelt of whiskey every time he visited me.

Mother detested him. She didn't say so. She never proclaimed detest out loud, but I always knew, and so did my father, when she was displeased with someone. Her pale blue eyes would ice over in the presence of such a person. When that happened, the detestee might as well have been exiled to the planet Mars, for Mother was, though a Christian and very loving, utterly unforgiving. Dr. Peavey was so exiled from her heart, mind, and soul.

But in spite of that, I got better. I could feel strength returning. I felt so chipper that I wrote Sergeant McCallum a letter, with my own hand.

*Dear Sergeant McCallum,*
    *How are you? How is the company?*
    *I have just about recovered from my wound.*
    *My mother came out from Rhode Island to tend to me. She has done an excellent job.*
    *What happened to Charolais, our little prairie flower from Lemon Corner? I do hope the authorities*

*will go easy on her. I don't believe she meant to shoot
me. She was just scared.*

*Please write me back if you can. And tell all the
boys hello for me.*

*Lt. M. Crofton*

And ten days later, I got a reply.

*Dere Lt,*

*The hoor excaped. We look for her for 2 days but
she disapert. You arnt ded. That's good. The company
has gont to hell. But we arnt ded.*

*Are you cumin bak?*

*McCallum*

An interesting question. Was I going back?

The quack doc who had been treating me said no. He
was recommending a medical discharge. Mother was satisfied with that. I wasn't.

"I owe two more years," I said.

"Honey," Mother said, "you are unable to serve."

"According to Dr. Know-Nothing?"

"And Dr. Stein."

It was a late-December evening, the sky darkening outside, a lamp lit near the bed. In the soft light of the lamp,
my mother looked worried.

Perhaps because of my youth, I had once again slipped

into my thoughts of immortality. I wasn't dead. I saw no reason I should be dead. And I didn't think I would, maybe ever, be dead. The bullet lodged in my body hadn't killed me, couldn't kill me. If anything, it was now a permanent talisman protecting me from death.

"Mama?" The old childhood word. "What will I do?"

"You'll come home. Dr. Stein will take the bullet out."

It was a close moment. All of what I had now of a life was there, at that moment.

"No," I said.

"Michael."

"It's my life," I said. "I will gain it or I will lose it. Either way, it's my choice."

Her nostrils flared, her eyes grew icy. Then a smile broke the hardness.

"There's some of your father in you," she said.

"Some," I said.

*Dear Son,*

    *Your mother tells me that you are recovering. I am most glad to hear that. You have been, constantly, in my prayers.*

    *I don't think I ever really believed you would die. Your mother would call that wishful thinking. And I grant that it was. But it had a kernel of reason to it. You are young. You are strong. And you got from your mother, if not from me, a hard and eternal inner core.*

*If you no longer need your madre, send her home, I do need her. This house is so lonesome. The dog mopes.*

*Do you need money? I have deposited a thousand dollars in an account for you at the Farmers and Merchants bank in Kansas City. You can draw on it when you like.*

*Your mother also tells me that you have broken off with Lucinda. Or that she broke off with you. I am very sorry. Sometimes God moves in mysterious ways, and I am sure He has plans for you.*

*You are, Michael, my always and ever loved son. Father*

Mother read the letter.

"I have to go," she said.

"I know," I said.

———

Mother stayed until Christmas day. The night before, Christmas Eve, we had a small party. Jeb brought hot cocoa, and Mother read the nativity story from the Bible. She and I didn't exchange gifts, but she did give Jeb the Bible as a gift. It somewhat perplexed the poor boy, for, as he told me after Mother had left, he couldn't read.

The next morning I gamely walked Mother to the door

of the infirmary and gave her a goodbye hug. There were tears in both our eyes.

"My dear boy," she said, dabbing at her eyes with a handkerchief.

"Mama," I said.

Then she was gone.

I slowly made my way back to my bed and collapsed into it, exhausted, from the exercise or the emotion, I could not determine which.

## VIII.

It was late February, and the wind out of the north was razor-cold. A little after noon, it began to sleet, and the icy pellets driven by the hard wind were like pinpricks in the clothing of the men and the hides of the animals.

I had been riding for three days with Cyrus Rill. He and three other men were driving a small herd of mules to Fort Hays out west. I had joined up with them in Fort Leavenworth. I was on my way to Fort Riley.

"There's an express station at Marysville," Rill said to me. He was riding next to me. Two Mexicans rode on either flank of the herd of mules, and a black man on a big gray mule rode in the front. The mules followed the big gray.

"We'll wait out the weather there," Rill said.

"How far?" I asked.

"Be there before dark."

I was miserable with the cold.

Dr. Peavey had certified me fit for duty. I had to threaten him to do it, but it didn't take much of a threat with a man like Peavey. In his medical career, he had long since passed any real care for his patients. His primary goal in life now was simply to avoid trouble.

I had drawn a spavined mare, bony as a rail. Her only consideration was that she was incapable of anything faster than a walk.

I wasn't sure I was prepared for duty. The bullet was still in my chest, though I was not really aware of it. What I was aware of was the thirty pounds I had lost. I was as thin as the nag I was riding, and the wind cut me like a knife.

It was only a half hour before dark when we arrived at the Pony Express station just east of the village of Marysville. The station proper was a mud and log cabin, one room, a barn out back, and a corral, into which Rill and his men drove the mules.

I stepped into the station. An old man sat smoking a pipe before a small lamp at a large plank table.

"Supper's a dollar," he said.

"How much for the warm?" I asked.

The old man didn't answer.

There was a fireplace on the east side of the room with a good fire. I moved to it and stood, warming my face and hands.

"That sleet out there," the old man said, "be snow by morning."

"What is that dollar supper?" I asked.

"Pea gravy," the old man said. "Got a little squirrel in it."

"Whiskey?"

" 'Nuther dollar."

And that was the meal. Two dollars for a bowl of pea gravy with a smidgen of squirrel and a cup of whiskey, but all in all, it was a fine repast. For another dollar, I got a spot on the floor near the fire, and within a half hour of digesting the fine meal, I was asleep.

The old man's prediction was correct. There was snow the next morning, a foot of it. There would be no traveling. For another dollar, I got flapjacks and coffee. Rill wouldn't pay. He ate hardtack and jerky, and the old man didn't charge him for sitting at the table with me.

The black and the two Mexicans had slept in the barn. The old man wouldn't allow them in the station.

Rill was an older fellow himself, long white hair and a beard just as white. I'd met him at Fort Leavenworth, where'd I been waiting a week for company on the trail. It wasn't country in which to travel alone. Rill had agreed to let me ride along with his remuda, though I had made clear to him that I was no mule skinner. I think he let me go because of my pistol. Twenty or so mules were a temptation, and should anybody attempt to take them, Rill could use an extra gun.

"You been to Hays?" Rill asked me.

"Yes."

"Two hundred miles from here, I reckon."

"Flat out there," I said. "Nothing to break the wind."

"What about Indians?" Rill asked.

"Possibility," I answered. "But this time of year, they're usually up in the mountains. They're smarter than we are."

"One of the reasons I'm doing this now."

"Better to fight snow and cold than Comanches."

The sky had cleared by afternoon, and the sunlight on the snow was blinding. It was bright sunshine, but still crinkly cold. Rill's hands came to the station for coffee, but then went back to the barn. Rill went out to them, came back and said they had a big fire going. That put the station master in a tizz, but Rill told him that he best let it be. His boys weren't going to sit out there and freeze.

"Where'd you get them goddam niggers?" the old station master asked.

"Only oncet a nigger."

"What's them other two?"

"Mescans."

"Mescans? Gawd almighty!"

"You best get used to it," Rill told him. "Niggers is free now, and Mescans are comin' north."

"Not here," said the old man. "We'll by God hang the sons of bitches."

Rill looked at me and grinned slightly. "Might as well not have fought the war with the South. Still too many peckerwoods."

"You in the war?" I asked.

"Ran mules for Grant at Vicksburg."

"He was something," I said.

"Man could drink," Rill said.

"I've heard that."

———— • ————

The station's barn burned down. Just before dark one of the Mexicans came banging on the station door, hollering in Spanish, and sure enough, the barn was blazing. There were a half-dozen horses stalled in it, but we managed to get them all out. What with the snow and the cold, we couldn't get water enough, and by dark, the barn was gone.

"You by God payin' for this!" the old geezer of a station master screamed at Rill.

"Like hell," Rill said.

It was dark and cold, and the embers of the barn put off a nice heat. The black and two Mexicans stood by, watching Rill, seeing how it would all play out.

"Yore men started it!" the station master hollered.

"It was an accident," Rill countered. "As much your fault as theirs."

"God damn it was!"

I walked up to the station master. "You let them sleep in the station, this wouldn't happen," I said.

"Ain't no goddamned niggers sleepin' with me!"

"You're out the barn, friend."

"We'll by God see about that," he said, stalking off.

We all stood close to the embered barn, catching its warmth, as the station master rode off through the snow on one of the horses. He was heading for the small settlement of Marysville to the west.

"He'll be back with men," I said to Rill.

"The Klan, most likely," Rill said.

The black man's head went up when he heard Rill say that.

Rill spoke to him: "Issac, get the guns, and you and them come into the station."

And so we barricaded ourselves.

The station had been built for just such an occasion, with heavy wooden window coverings all around that propped open from the inside. They served as excellent gun ports. The five of us situated ourselves around the large room, each man at a port.

"You needn't stay for this," Rill said to me. "This ain't your fight."

"Where am I going to go?" I said. "A foot of snow out there and my horse useless."

"There will be killing."

"I've seen killing."

I had my pistol, a .44 caliber Colt, and thirty cartridges. Rill gave me a Sharps rifle and a dozen bullets. It was a single-shot, lever-action, a .50 caliber, heavy and steady.

"Hit sumthin' a mile way wid dat," Issac said to me. He had a Winchester.

KEITH COPLIN

So did the two Mexicans.

Rill cooked up some pea soup and found some hard bread. He also poured out whiskey from a big white jug. We took turns eating, two eating, two watching the windows.

"Not too much of that whiskey, boys," Rill said.

Later, Rill and I sat at the table.

"Where you from?" he asked me.

"Rhode Island."

"You don't say?"

"You?"

"Missoura," Rill said. "Bet you wish you was back in Rhode Island 'bout now."

"No. I'm where I want to be."

"Soldierin' long?"

"Six years. It's my profession."

Rill had made some coffee, and he sipped some from his cup.

"They'll get here before dawn," he said. "Won't do nothin' long as it's dark. They'll shoot awhile, then they'll burn us out."

"Why do you think it will be the Klan?" I asked.

"'Cause of Issac."

"Do your boys shoot well?"

"Well enough."

It was two men up for two hours, then two more for another two hours. I didn't take a watch. Rill insisted that I not. He knew I wasn't completely up to snuff. And the fact is, I could feel a grating in my chest. The huffing and puffing from getting the horses out of the burning barn had put me in a state, my chest aching. I slept by the fire, my pistol near my head.

———

Men had come during the night. It was dreadfully cold, and I wondered how many of them really wanted to be there.

"How many?" I asked Rill.

"Twenty," he said. "Maybe a few more."

I had waked up and stood next to Rill now, a cup of hot coffee in my hand. Rill was looking out the window next to the front door. It faced south.

"Mistah Rill?" Issac said from the back.

"Yeah?"

"They gittin' round behind us here. Fo' of 'em."

"*Aqui,*" said the Mexican on the east wall. "*Tres.*"

"Manuel?" Rill said to the Mexican at the west window.

"*Dos,*" he said.

"Put down the shutters, boys, and stand away from the windows," Rill said.

And the shooting started.

We all huddled on the floor, away from the walls and windows. We could hear the bullets thudding into the heavy wooden window shutters and into the log-and-mud walls. But none of them came inside. The gunfire was steady, and I tried to count the number of guns, but there were too many. I had turned the big wooden table sideways and sat behind it, my back to the fireplace, in which a small fire smoldered.

The gunfire intensified, then began to fade away. After about twenty minutes, the shooting stopped.

"There," Rill said. "They through jackin' off."

Then the gunfire picked up again.

"Oh, Lawd," Issac said. "They shootin' de mules."

And we could hear the horrible braying of the dying animals.

Rill went to Issac's window and opened the shutter just a bit. He had a .30/.30 Winchester, and he poked it through the opening, fired, cocked, and fired again. He got off six quick shots, then dropped the shutter with a bang.

"Sons of bitches," he said.

Issac peeked out. "You done kilt three of 'em, Mistah Rill."

There was a fusillade of shots then, striking the building at all angles.

Above the gunfire, Rill said, "Wait until the shooting dies down, boys, then open your windows and shoot to kill. Kill every one of the peckerwood bastards."

When the shooting died down, that's exactly what we tried to do.

I knocked one man down at a good hundred yards with the Sharps. The rifle had a wallop of a kick. Back of me, the cabin roared with rifle fire. I missed a fellow at fifty yards.

He was down behind a snowbank, and though I missed him, I was sure I'd scared Jesus into him. When we ran out of targets, we stopped shooting.

"Manuel?" Rill called.

"*Dos.*"

"Hector?" Rill called to the other Mexican.

"*Uno. Chinga!*"

"I shot one," Issac reported.

"I got one," I said.

Rill didn't say how many he got. But he did say, "We either made them real mad or we discouraged them something fierce."

———·———

They doused the south side of the cabin with coal oil that night. We smelt it, a heavy, vaporous fume that set me to coughing. They managed to sneak up close in the darkness.

Rill said there was nothing we could do about it. The snow on the roof would help us a little, but when they lighted the south wall come morning, it would burn proper, the wood having soaked all night.

We discussed sneaking out, making a run for it, but Rill reasonably pointed out that our horses were scattered, and even if we got by the men in the darkness, they could easily track us in the snow. Our best chance was to wait for the burn, then shoot them as they came in. If we could get enough of them, then we could go out the wall and shoot from outside. The heavier the price they had to pay, the more likely they would give up and go.

Come daylight, the wall began to burn. Soon the cabin began to fill with smoke. I lay flat on the floor, but the coal oil fumes and the smoke from the damp logs in the wall were suffocating. I began to cough, every spasm a tear at my chest. Soon a fine spray of blood accompanied each heave.

The wall began to collapse within an hour, and they came.

I fired blindly with my pistol, in the general direction of the open wall, but between the smoke and my coughing and the incessant gunfire inside the cabin, all was chaos. The noise was deafening. When I had emptied my revolver, I curled up behind the overturned table and reloaded. Then I was up again and firing.

Finally, there was a lull, and I heard Rill.

"Outside, boys! Go through the wall. Stay low and keep shooting!"

But I could not obey. I was seized by enormous, racking coughs, on all fours, head down, retching between each mighty heave, feeling my lungs, as if they were ripping, then a terrible, horrible movement in my chest, unable to breathe, my wind gone, choking, and in utter desperation, I heaved, vomit, bile, one mighty push from my innards, and amidst the wet and mess, the bullet, the whore's bullet, there on the floor.

And then I passed out.

———

"Praise de Lawd!"

"Lieutenant?"

"Done give us a mighty victory! Praise Jesus!"

"Lieutenant?"

I opened my eyes to bright sunshine, and I felt the cold, clean air, washing over me and touching my face, like cool, soft fingers.

I was lying on a buffalo robe spread on the snow. Rill was knelt down beside me. Issac was standing, his face up to the sun.

"What happened?" I asked.

"We whipped 'em," Rill said.

"Hector? Manuel?"

"Gone to fetch horses. They're scattered, but those boys can get 'em."

"The Klan?"

"What ain't dead is gone."

"I'm sorry," I said.

"What?"

"I passed out."

"You killed three, with your pistol," Rill said. "The first three in."

"Rill?"

"What?"

"In the cabin," I said, weakly. "Where I passed out. On the floor. 'Midst the mess . . ."

"Yes?"

"A bullet. Will you fetch it for me?"

## IX.

"GAWD, Lieutenant, you look like shit."

"Nice to see you, too, McCallum."

I was propped up in a sentry's hut at the west gate to Fort Riley. McCallum was standing above me. The gate guard was gone to fetch an ambulance.

It had taken me a week to ride from Marysville to Fort Riley.

McCallum asked, "You been shot?"

"No."

I had arrived at the west gate of the fort and been challenged by the sentry. I'd told him to get McCallum, then slid unconscious from my horse. When I came to, I was in the hut, McCallum tending me. I was terribly thirsty.

"McCallum?"

"Aye?"

"There will be trouble. From Marysville. I was never there. I was here."

"Aye."

And then I went to sleep. I was awfully tired.

———

There wasn't a full-time doctor at the fort. There was a doctor, but he rode circuit, Fort Larned, Fort Dodge, Fort Hays, and Fort Riley. He was at Larned at the time. But I did have a medical orderly, Corporal Sytes, the aid man who had staunched my bleeding at Lemon Corner.

"Frostbite," the corporal said. "Both feet. But you won't lose no toes. You pretty dried out, though."

"I'm hungry," I said.

We were in the infirmary. It was small, only three other beds, two of them occupied.

"Put some soup in you," Sytes said. "Water, too. You are dehydrated."

"I ate snow."

"Not enough."

Sytes washed my feet with warm water and soap, then put some ointment on them.

"Corporal? Did McCallum talk to you?"

"Yes, sir. You been here two weeks."

The soup was good, heavy beef broth, bits of meat floating in it. I had a quick bowl, but Sytes wouldn't let me have another. He made me drink water instead.

My second day, a colonel came to see me, the fort's adjutant. I didn't know him.

"Lawson," he said, standing next to my bed. "Colonel Lawson."

"Sir."

"Seems you had quite a trip from Fort Leavenworth."

"Yes, sir."

"And you've been here how long?"

"Two weeks, sir."

"I see," he said, fidgeting with his gloves. He glanced out the window. "Did you come by way of Marysville?"

"No, sir."

Again he fidgeted with his gloves.

"Well, Lieutenant, you take care of yourself."

"Yes, sir," I said. "I will."

Then he left.

That afternoon, McCallum came to see me.

"Gawd almighty, Lieutenant!" He had pulled up a stool and sat next to my bed. "They's fifteen dead citizens up at Marysville."

I said nothing.

"It's in the newspaper," McCallum said. "Some mule skinner and a band of renegade blacks. Killed 'em and got off with their horses."

"Tragic," I said.

"Says there was an army man with 'em."

"Did it say the dead men were with the Klan?" I asked.

McCallum looked at me. "No," he said, "it didn't say that."

McCallum sat pensively for a while. I shut my eyes.

"I'll be going, Lieutenant."

"All right," I said, not opening my eyes. I heard McCallum get up, move the stool. "Sergeant?"

"Sir?"

"That horse, the one I rode in on."

"What horse, sir?"

My eyes still closed, I smiled. "I think I'll take a little nap."

"Be good for you, Lieutenant," McCallum said.

———

"What of the whore?"

"Escaped."

It was my fifth day in the Fort Riley infirmary, and McCallum had brought me a jar of pickles. They were home-canned pickles, put up by a Mrs. Trotter, a widow woman who lived down the road from the fort.

"She just walked away?"

"Now, Lieutenant, you have got to try one of these pickles. Mrs. Trotter says they are her best batch yet."

It was Sunday afternoon, and McCallum was wearing his dress uniform.

"Why are you dressed up?" I asked.

"I been to church."

"Church?"

McCallum dug out a pickle and made a show of eating it.

I said, "I had no idea you were religious, Sergeant."

"It's the Widow Trotter who is religious."

"Widow?"

"A fine Christian woman."

"Who makes delicious pickles," I said.

"Have one, Lieutenant," he said, offering me the opened jar. "They'll take you back to your childhood."

Of course, I ate one.

"The whore," I said, my pickle half eaten.

McCallum started on another pickle, then pulled a huge rag from his tunic and dabbed at his mouth.

"The day after we sent you back to Fort Riley," he said. He offered me the jar again. "Another?"

"No," I said, gesturing with my half pickle, "thank you."

"Well," he continued, "there was a lot of confusion. You know, two of them fellows died, them ones in the saloon. We dug eight graves. Oh, it was a sight."

"Sergeant."

"Gone."

"What?"

"She was gone."

"The whore?"

"Yes, sir."

"You didn't have a guard on her?" I asked.

"Well, yes, we did. But I reckon she slipped by him." McCallum chewed, swallowed. "In the night."

Corporal Sytes came in with a pitcher of water.

"Corporal?" I said.

"Sir?"

"What happened to the whore?"

"We let her go."

"Harrummmph!" McCallum made a sound, a throat sound. He jumped to his feet. "Have you tried one of these pickles?" he asked Sytes, making a menacing look with his face.

Sytes suddenly looked burdened.

"Sit down, Sergeant," I said. "Sytes, put that pitcher on the table here."

He did.

"Now," I said, "I want the story."

McCallum was using his big rag to wipe his reddening face.

I looked directly at the corporal. "What do you mean you let her go?" He looked at McCallum. "Don't look at him," I said. "Look at me."

"It was his idea," Sytes said, nodding at McCallum.

"By my mother's eyes . . ." McCallum muttered.

"Hush, Sergeant," I said. "What do you mean, it was his idea?" I asked Sytes.

"Lettin' her go," the corporal said. "We had a troop meetin'. The sergeant, he put it to a vote."

"To let her go?"

"Yes, sir."

"And what was the result of the vote?"

"Nary a no," Sytes said. "Though we all felt bad she shot you."

"Lieutenant?" McCallum said.

"Hush." Then, to the corporal: "When you got back here to Riley, what did your report say?"

"That she escaped," Sytes said.

"Did the major or anyone order you to look for her?"

"No, sir."

"So where is she?" I asked. "Whorin' in Abilene? Dodge?"

"No, sir," Sytes said. "We made her promise to quit whorin' afore we let her go."

"Ah," I said. "A whore's promise. Good as gold."

"Lieutenant?" It was McCallum. He had a pleading look on his face.

"You know something, McCallum?" I said. "You could be court-martialed for this, drummed out of the army."

"Sir? She's a child."

"With how many men dead because of her?"

"Warn't no fault of hers," McCallum said. "And shootin' you? She probably thought you was a Texan. I tell you, Lieutenant, if you could have seen her, after."

"After what?"

"After all the hubbub."

I put my half-eaten pickle on the table next to the bed.

"Where is she?" I asked.

McCallum looked at Sytes. Sytes looked at McCallum.

"That, Lieutenant," McCallum said, "I couldn't tell you."

I looked at the corporal. "Sytes?" I said.

"Believe me, sir, when I last seen her, she was in that tent lookin' forlorn and sad."

"God," I said, "a cavalry of fools."

## X.

IT HAD taken what seemed a lifetime to get back to my quarters at Fort Riley. The unmarried officers' billet consisted of a two-story building quartered into individual rooms, up and down. Since I was, with almost two years at Riley, a senior lieutenant, I had a ground-floor, corner room. It had been used, of course, during my absence, but it was mine now, and I luxuriated in its possession.

The room was, really, quite Spartan: a cot, a washstand, a small table, a chair, and a lamp. But this March afternoon it was, to me, as posh as a suite at the Hôtel de Paris. I stretched out on the stiff cot in grand comfort, thankful at last not to be in an infirmary.

And studied the bullet.

The .42 caliber slug fired from the whore's derringer, a ball really, but no longer honest in its circumference. It had flattened a bit when it hit my breastplate, but it hadn't shattered. Had it broken up, it would have been like shrapnel exploding inside my chest, the fragments ripping and tearing every which way. But it had stayed intact, a fixed solid, and, as I studied it in the pale late-winter light from the window, it looked now like a small, lopsided marble.

In and now out, an epic journey, death-defying, and . . . the revelation of the bullet . . . luck.

"They have the man, Rill, in Kansas City."

"He's been arrested?"

My day of reckoning had arrived. I had been summoned to the office of General Seavers, commandant of Fort Riley. The general sat now, behind his desk, and I sat stiffly across from him in a high-backed, hard chair.

"Not exactly," the general said. "He's being detained."

"By whom?" I asked.

"The authorities."

I wanted to ask which authorities, but I reasoned that this might be a good time not to talk at all.

Seavers eyed me for a bit. He was a general in the U.S. Army, and as such, the current situation forced him to consider not only his duty as a soldier but his skill as a politician.

"Rill claims," he said, "that the Ku Klux Klan was involved." He waited for me to respond, and when I didn't, he continued. "He also claims that no Army personnel were involved."

Now I needed to say something.

"What, exactly, General, does this have to do with me?"

"That, Lieutenant, you must explain to me."

"There's nothing to explain, sir."

Again, that hawklike look.

Seavers, I knew, was career Army, a graduate of West Point, like me. He had commanded a regiment under Phil Sheridan during the war, and his reputation as a commander was unsoiled. He would rise through the ranks at a steady, predictable pace, never perceived of as brilliant, but always thought of as competent.

It occurred to me, sitting there at what could have been a tense moment, that Seavers was Horatio to Custer's Hamlet.

Finally, the general spoke: "There is not a lot of Klan activity in this area."

"Not anymore," I said.

———

Thus the matter was closed. The Army had taken care of its own. It was as I had surmised. Sentiment against the Klan, particularly in the Army, was the deciding factor. Those weren't citizens who had been gunned down in Marysville. They were Klansmen. In the broader scheme of things, they had simply gotten what they deserved.

Of course, I would now have an invisible mark against my name. I'd been in the service long enough to realize that indeed the Army did take care of its own, but the Army never forgot either. Nothing would ever appear on paper. I would be merely a topic of conversation, a whiskey subject for late-night chatter. And unless there was another mammoth war in the future, I'd never make general.

McCallum, who had been in the Army longer than I had, thought I'd be transferred.

"Soiled linen," he said.

"Not an apt metaphor, Sergeant," I said.

"Sir?"

He and I sat on the front porch of the officers' billet. It was a heady, near-spring afternoon, the sky a keen azure that made the eye ache.

"Yes, sir," McCallum said. "Soiled linen. They'll wash you out in some godforsaken place, Alabama maybe."

"Any Indians in Alabama?'

"No, sir. They moved them all to Oklahoma, I think."

"Lots of Rebs, though."

"There's that," McCallum said.

McCallum was whittling a stick, the shavings dropping in soft curls to the porch's plank floor.

"What of you, Sergeant? What are your plans?"

"Plans?"

"Surely you don't intend to stay in the Army forever."

McCallum stared off across the compound, a wistful look on his face.

"I'm marryin'," he said.

"What?"

"If the Widow Trotter will have me."

"And the Army?"

"Gittin' out."

"After how many years?" I asked.

"Too many," McCallum said.

Thus I was recruited to serve as McCallum's chaperone. That's not the word he used, but that was his intent. Though I think, too, the sergeant wanted to demonstrate to the Widow Trotter that he was of a civilized disposition, my accompanying him evidence of that.

We arrived at the widow's house on the following Saturday afternoon, both of us dressed formally. It was but a short walk from the fort, and though the day was bright and sunny, there was a breeze out of the north that gave it a bit of a chill.

McCallum never said a word as we walked. I could tell that he was full of a kind of elevated apprehension, his steps stiff and jerky, his eyes trained levelly ahead. He carried a bouquet. I had suggested that. They were wildflowers, picked off the gunnery range at the fort, but they had color and intent. I didn't know if McCallum had previously discussed matrimony with the Widow Trotter, but I suspected he hadn't.

"At ease, sergeant," I said, as we approached the widow's house.

He looked at me, a look forlorn in its helplessness.

I said, "The worst that can happen is that she will say no."

"It ain't the no that's worrying me," he said. "It's the yes."

The Widow Trotter was a formidable woman, not fat exactly, but stout. She greeted us at her front door. She wore a gray dress, and her hair was up, in a bun. She had gray eyes, quite becoming, and made even grayer by the dress.

"Gentlemen," she said, greeting us.

McCallum offered her the flowers, much as a child would offer a gift to an adult.

"Why, Lionel," she said. "You shouldn't have."

Lionel? I had never, in the time I had known McCallum, heard him addressed by his first name.

"Mavis," McCallum said, "this is Lieutenant Crofton."

"Lieutenant," she said.

"Ma'am."

"Please, both of you. Come in. Mind. Wipe your feet."

———

Sergeant Lionel McCallum, a longtime veteran of the U.S. Army, a decorated soldier, a credit to the nation and (apparently) a reformed drunk, was as clumsy as a schoolboy in church. He literally couldn't speak.

We sat, the sergeant, Widow Trotter, and I, in her parlor, drinking tea. McCallum had already fumbled one cup, dropping it disastrously on the floor, where, thank heaven, it didn't break. And he was now nursing his second cup as carefully as a mother with an infant, not daring to drink from it, but holding it in his big paw.

"Rhode Island," the widow said. "Where exactly is that?"

"Back east," I said. "Part of New England, south of Boston."

"Ah," said the widow.

"And you're from Kansas?" I asked.

"I'm originally from Illinois," she said. "Mr. Trotter and I came out here after the war. He intended to farm."

"Illinois is nice," I said.

McCallum was suffocating. His tunic was buttoned to the top button, and his face was turning a darker and darker shade of red and brown.

"I'm not sure where the sergeant is from," I said, turning to McCallum for some kind of sign. "Originally. Where were you raised, Sergeant?"

"Mrs. Trotter," he said, his voice heavy with a sudden expiration of air. "I've come to ask your hand."

I swear, the look on his face was one of sheer terror.

"Oh?" the Widow Trotter said.

Then the room was deadly quiet. I said nothing. McCallum said nothing. The Widow Trotter said nothing.

The tension was relieved by the entrance of a young woman.

"Louise," said Mrs. Trotter, rising. "Come in, come in, child."

McCallum struggled to his feet, and I rose too.

"Gentlemen, my niece, Louise."

McCallum had now gone white.

"This is Lieutenant Crofton," Mrs. Trotter said to

Louise, gesturing to me. "And I think you know Sergeant McCallum."

"Hello," the girl said.

She was wearing a long beige skirt with a matching blouse high up her neck. Her blond hair was tied back. But I knew the eyes, blue and clear. She'd put on a little weight.

McCallum fainted, dead away.

## XI.

MCCALLUM HAD been at Cold Harbor. The night before the final Union attack, soldiers had pinned their names on the back of their tunics so their bodies could be identified. A man who would face that was no coward. It took a woman to turn McCallum into a sissy.

Yet his fainting, unbeknownst to him, had been a grand tactic. The Widow Trotter was obviously moved. She tended him in the parlor after I had lifted the heft of him into a chair.

Lionel McCallum had lied to me. He knew the whereabouts of the whore, though I could assume she was no longer in the profession. He had either forgotten about her being at the widow's house in all the hubbub of his matrimonial plans, or her appearance was not part of the plan. Had he fainted because his lie was exposed? I think not. He fainted from love. McCallum was a fool of the best kind, a fool for love.

Louise and I now sat on the front porch, on a step. The cool morning had become a warm afternoon. We sat in the sun, its warmth a comfort.

It had all become clear to me as the Widow Trotter and I waited for the sergeant to recover. She explained. McCallum had brought Louise to her, a frail little thing, and had explained to the widow the girl's poor circumstance. The Widow Trotter, with no children of her own, took the girl, and she and McCallum had concocted the story about Louise being the widow's niece.

"Will he be all right?" Louise asked.

"Yes," I said.

We sat side by side, and occasionally I would glance over at her. She had a fine aristocratic neck, and her hair, piled in a bun, was the color of ripe wheat.

"How old are you?" I asked.

"I don't know," she said. "I was never told."

"McCallum brought you here?"

"Yes."

"And the Widow Trotter has looked after you?"

"She brought me to Jesus," Louise said.

"Well," I said, looking down the flagstone walk that led to the road, "that's a good thing."

"Did I shoot you?"

"Yes."

She was quiet a few seconds, then said, "I thought you were a cowboy."

"You didn't kill me," I said.

Then she looked along the flagstone walk and at the greening field across the road.

"I meant to," she said.

"This was before you were brought to Jesus."

"Yes."

"So I assume you wouldn't want to kill me now."

"No. Are you with Jesus?"

"Undoubtedly," I said, aware, for the instant, of Louise's bullet in the pocket of my pants.

A strand of hair had come loose and fell down onto Louise's forehead. She brushed it back and said, "Mrs. Trotter is teaching me to read."

"That's wonderful."

"I'm reading the Bible."

"That's pretty hard reading," I said.

"I get the thees and the thous mixed up."

As I sat with her, I tried to think of what she was. An orphan? An urchin? A wild thing growing on the prairie? But all I could finally determine was that she was young, pretty, and somehow voraciously alive.

"Where are you from?" I asked.

She looked at me, and for the first time her beautiful eyes didn't seem hard or businesslike.

"All over," she said. "My daddy was a traveling man."

"And your mother?"

"She died."

"Ah."

"Daddy died, too," Louise said. "Big Jim killed him."

"Big Jim?"

"At Lemon Corner."

And I remembered, Big Jim Clancey, the saloon owner, the first man the Texans had killed.

"Why did he kill him?" I asked.

"To get me."

"What do you mean, to get you?"

"Daddy had bet me in a poker hand. Daddy won. He had three aces."

"Big Jim didn't like the outcome of the game," I said.

"No. He shot Daddy, then made me a whore."

This was grotesque news, and I sat for a moment, trying to calm the clammy, cold feeling that was rising in me.

"How did you feel about that?" I asked. "Being Big Jim's whore?"

"I didn't like it," she said. "But I pretended I did. Big Jim said he'd kill me if I didn't pretend."

She sat with both hands folded on her lap. I sat next to her, my boots stretched out in front of me. The afternoon lay like a big, yellow, lazy cat on the spring-green yard and fields beyond.

## XII.

THE WIDOW TROTTER and Sergeant McCallum were married in the Rocky Creek Baptist Church on the first of

June. It was a small wedding. I stood up for the sergeant. Louise stood up for the widow.

The next day, I was ordered to report to the War Department in Washington for reassignment. I was being transferred out of the 7th Cavalry.

I helped the sergeant move his personal things from the fort to the house he would now share with Mrs. McCallum. When all was moved, he stood with me on the front porch of the house.

"They'll put you behind a desk," McCallum said, "and keep you there until you learn you can't side with civilians and kill white men wholesale."

"And you, Sergeant," I said, "what will they do with you now that you're an old married man?"

"They ain't doin' squat to me. Come July one, I'm a civilian. Thirty years I was in this man's army. Fourteen battle stars. I've served."

"And Louise?"

"What of her?" he asked.

"I'm taking her with me, Sergeant," I said.

"Are you now?"

"Yes," I said. "I am."

———

She seemed to understand the situation perfectly.

"So you will come with me?" I asked.

"Yes," she said.

"We'll have to marry."

We were walking down the road, a couple in a late-spring idyll. It was evening, the landscape mellow and a light orange with the waning sun.

"Will you help me?" she asked.

"With what?"

"Reading."

"Of course," I said.

## Two

## I.

WASHINGTON IN late June 1877 was sweltering. The War Department on 17th Street was an oven.

"Good God, man, how do you stand this?"

He looked at me, the little second lieutenant from Michigan, his blue tunic buttoned all the way up, and grinned. His name was Sorensen.

"Baked beans," he said.

I liked the little squirrel, though he had this irritating quality of not sweating. No matter how hot it was, he never removed his tunic, perspiration droplets never popped out on his forehead or upper lip, and he never complained of the heat. He was a congressional second lieutenant, meaning that he'd come of his commission via his father, who was a representative from some little-known congressional district in northern Michigan. But he was a good fellow, and he treated Louise and me with benign acceptance and even provided Louise with *McGuffey's Reader*, a handsome little booklet for beginners.

His job, as mine, was to coordinate pistols and rifles with armories throughout the United States. In other words, we found places to put the guns out of harm's way. The soldiers who would use the guns were disappearing at an alarming rate. The army was dwindling.

"Sorensen," I said, "why do you never sweat?"

We both sat at a double desk, across from each other.

"Salt," he said.

"Salt?"

"I eat salt."

"Just straight salt," I said.

"Yep."

I looked at him, a drop of sweat blurring my vision as it made its way through my eyebrow and into the recess of my tired eye.

"You're a hopeless little tadpole," I said.

"Three hundred Colt pistols, caliber forty-four." He handed me a sheet of paper across the two desks. "Origin Yazoo City, Mississippi. Need a home."

"We could give them to the blacks," I said.

"Make Yazoo City safer for everyone," he said.

Federal troops, stationed throughout the South during the period of Reconstruction, were withdrawing. The War of the Rebellion was, finally, over. Grant was out of the White House, and civilians were popping up everywhere.

"They won, you know," Sorensen said.

"Who won?"

"The Klan."

"You think?"

"Yep."

I studied the inventory he had handed me. "Then we ought to give guns to the blacks."

"Indeed," said Sorensen.

"Hey, Sorensen."

"Sir?"

"You ever shot a gun?"

He turned his head this way, then that. "Nope," he said.

"Not even in training?"

"Nope."

"You want one of these Colts?"

"Nope."

At the bottom of the inventory sheet, I printed: *Jefferson, St. Louis.*

"Well, there they are," I said. "Locked up in the closet."

"Score another one for the Klan," Sorensen said.

It was the nation's capital for Louise and me. We had a small house on M Street, only blocks from the War Department. It wasn't much of a house, three rooms and a privy out back. But for us it was the honeymoon suite. We'd been married almost a month, married by a justice of the peace in St. Charles, Missouri, on our way to D.C.

We had consummated our marriage in a sleeper of the Cincinnati-bound Union Pacific. Louise hadn't uttered a word, and had even been shy and withdrawn, but by the time we got to Pittsburgh, she'd overcome that. She was a hot little potato, and when she finally realized that she didn't have to pretend anymore, she didn't.

"And this is all right?" she had asked, demurely.

"Husband and wife," I said, "Adam and Eve, praise Jesus."

If it was all right with Jesus, I knew, it would be all right with Louise.

There was some extraneous paperwork on our arrival in Washington. The Army had not accounted for my being a married man, but since I was assigned to the War Department, I had been able to expedite that situation, and within two weeks, Louise and I had the blessing not only of the state and church but of the U.S. Army as well. I even got an extra twenty-five dollars a month in pay, which more than covered the rent on our little abode of marital bliss.

I walked to work every morning a new man, my fur shining.

And the work, demeaning, boring, hot. I was chained to a desk, just as McCallum had predicted. I was expected to be in the little cubbyhole of an office at 8 A.M., and I had to stay there until 4 P.M., and some weekends I drew duty guarding the White House. My immediate superior was a Captain Lucius Allen, a spit-and-polish D.C. soldier a year younger than me and bound for better things.

Sorensen and I called Allen "Napoleon" behind his back. First of all, the captain was short, shorter even than Sorensen, who was really short. Second, Allen was West Point, without the leavening of field duty. He'd come from the Point directly to D.C., and since his father was a brigadier general, stationed in New York, of all places, our little martinet captain was a toy soldier bound for bureaucratic glory.

My second day of duty, Captain Allen jumped me about my buttons.

"My buttons, sir?" I said, standing at attention behind my already cluttered desk.

"Cloudy," Captain Allen said.

"Sir?"

"Your buttons are cloudy."

"Yes, sir."

"See to it, Lieutenant. We're not at some horse post, you know."

Sorensen loaned me some mustache wax (perfect, he said, for polishing buttons), and I shaped up, so to speak.

But I had a few delicious thoughts of Allen being dealt with by Comanches. They'd destarch him, pronto.

But all in all, life was good.

Except supper was boiled potatoes, no butter, no salt.

"Louise?"

She looked at me, my little mouse. She wore a wrap-around, Indian-style, a blanket actually, but even in that, she looked scrumptious.

"What?" she said with questioning eyes.

"We really can afford to eat a bit better than this."

"What's wrong with potatoes?" she asked.

"Nothing. Potatoes are great. When they're served with something else—meat, for instance. And even green beans."

"My daddy never complained about my cooking," she said.

I had a wild little prairie thing here, of that I was aware. There were no fine edges on this woman. She knew about sex, more or less. She had been rough schooled in that. And she knew about survival. A daddy who would bet her in a card game had left her on her own at a very early age. And she knew about shooting people. She'd shot at least two. But on account, that was just about the sum of her knowledge.

But like all wild things, she had an enormous capacity for living. That, finally, was what I loved about her. And there's the word: love. I hadn't thought much about that word, had never mentioned it to her. I'd never heard her use it, either. I don't think she really knew what it meant. I was dead certain that until I came along, no one had ever loved her. So how could she know?

But I knew. She was my heart's desire. And would be until the day I died.

"Put on your dress," I said. "We're going out."

"What for?"

"To eat," I said.

And she put a pout on her pretty little face.

———·——

Ulysses S. Grant, former head of the Union Army and ex–President of the United States, said, "Cuba."

"Five hundred rifles," I said.

"Yes."

"Fifty-seven caliber Enfields, muzzle loaders."

"That's right."

Sorensen was frozen with fear.

I said, "They will be shipped from the armory at Harpers Ferry to Orlando, Florida." I looked at the paper before me, then back at Grant. "And there will be no record of transfer. How will they get into Cuba?"

"Sheridan will see to it," Grant said.

And with that, the ex-President left the office.

I sat down. So did Sorensen.

Ulysses S. Grant had walked into Sorensen's and my office at a little after ten in the morning on a Tuesday in the first week of July, and he had handed me a slip of paper on which was written: "Ordnance, Harpers Ferry, fifty-seven cal, five hundred."

The general said to wire an order to have the rifles shipped to Orlando, with a further order to destroy the wire. There would be no record of transfer. Grant wore civilian clothes, a dark suit. His beard was trimmed. And he wore a hat.

Sorensen and I stared at each other.

"Do you want to send the wire?" I asked.

He shook his head no.

"I'll do it," I said, and I got up to do it.

Later, Sorensen and I sat in the tavern attached to the Murray Hotel, just two blocks from our office. We were drinking two glasses of warm beer. And Sorensen, for the first time I had ever noticed, was sweating.

"Jesus," he said.

"I guess they aim to kill the Spanish bastards," I said.

It was known, but not well known, in Army circles that the United States was arming Cuban rebels fighting the Spanish in Cuba.

"Jesus," Sorensen said again.

"What are you Jesusing about?" I asked. "It was just Grant."

Sorensen started to say Jesus again, but didn't.

"Anyway," I said. "Those Enfields are obsolete."

When he'd finished his beer, Sorensen more or less got himself back together.

"You're going to Rhode Island?" he asked.

"Next week," I said. "I got two weeks' leave."

"I didn't know he was so short."

"Grant?"

"Yeah."

"Knew what he was about, though, didn't he?"

"We can't tell anybody about this, can we?"

"No." I sipped my beer. "Sorensen?"

"Yeah?"

"You're sweating."

"No shit," Sorensen said.

## II.

IT HAD BEEN more than two years since I'd been in New York. And it seemed larger. The hustle, the bustle, the noise and crowds, the streets jammed with wagons and carriages, I now saw them as a country boy would. Louise clung to me, frightened out of her wits. We'd arrived in the afternoon on the train from Washington, two bumpkins in Baghdad. We walked from the station to the Belmont Hotel, a place I knew from my days at the Point. The four blocks were a stroll through wonderland. I'd never seen Louise's eyes so big.

"It's the city, darling," I said to her as we neared the hotel.

"It's awful," she said.

But our room at the Belmont was wonderful, with a big brass bed and a water closet (Louise pulled the latch on it and watched with absolute amazement as the water funneled out). We put our belongings away, then rode the elevator down from our floor, another act of magic that left Louise utterly bewildered, and then, on Fifth Avenue, we shopped.

I'd closed out my account at the Farmers and Merchants bank in Kansas City on our trip to the East, and I had now eight hundred greenback American dollars, which I splurged on my beautiful young wife. Millinery, dress, gown, jacket, brocade and silk, satin collars, lace-up boots, it was a gloriously materialistic afternoon, with dainty clerks cruising to our every whim, and stern, corseted store managers arranging outfits according to my lady's need and color. It was marvelous, a transcendent transformation of girl to woman, topped, at afternoon's end, by a ring, actually a ring set, engagement and wedding band, purchased with low-key abandon at Tiffany's.

"What's it for?" Louise asked me.

"It's a tradition," I said. "It indicates to the world that you are married." I kissed her cheek. "To me."

"It cost a lot of money," she said. "You could buy a good rifle with that kind of money."

We had dinner at Delmonico's, and a bottle of champagne. The bubbles from the wine tickled Louise's nose and made her giggle. A hansom cab took us back to the hotel, and in the big brass bed we slept the sleep of angels, tucked deliciously into each other's arms.

Providence, home, the city stately and not so stately, but old, by American standards, rivaling Boston. I had wired my parents that I was coming, and I had mentioned that I was bringing someone with me, but I hadn't had the courage to say who. It was a dicey situation. Father would accept Louise. I had no doubt of that. But Mother, well, it would take her not more than two minutes to figure out who Louise was. I had thought, and thought even now, that a *fait accompli* was the best strategy with *ma mère*.

Louise could not get over all the water. From New York on the train, we'd been in sight of water almost the whole trip. She had no experience with oceans, and the Atlantic was a sweet mystery to her. When I told her it was three thousand miles across, she was speechless.

On arrival in Providence, I hired a carriage cab and driver at the train station, and Louise and I commenced the trip to Wynamore Street, on which my parents lived. The closer we got, the more of my old life came hurtling back. There was the public library where I'd had my first library card, the grade school I'd attended, Shapiro's Bakery, where I'd consumed many a roll, Tri-State Suitry, where I'd been outfitted for my suit upon graduating from high school. It all seemed so familiar, yet so distant in the past. I could feel myself drawing up, pulling away from memory yet irresistibly drawn toward it.

As the carriage stopped in front of my parents' house, I was seized with a strange and powerful doubt. The ride from the train station to this street had been a journey of pure nostalgia. But now I had not a sense of home, but an uncanny sense of not belonging. This place was not where Louise and I belonged.

"Your parents live here?" Louise asked, her voice pulling me up from deep within myself.

I turned my head to look at her, then I turned again to look at the house.

"Yes."

"Is your father a president?"

I smiled, turned again to her. "Yes, in a way."

It wasn't an imposing house. I should take Louise to see the houses at Newport. She would think those belonged to kings. But Mr. Harold Crofton's house was splendid, in a richly middle-class way. Though, oddly, I had never thought so until now.

When the carriage was gone, Louise and I stood on the sidewalk that ran parallel to the street for the length of the block. Louise eyed it with wonder. I held two big bags. Louise had a small one.

There was a rock walk up to the small front porch of the house, and I looked at it as I would look at a pathway into an unknown wood. Louise didn't say anything, just stood next to me.

We moved as one up the walk to the house.

My father answered the door. It was, I realized, a Sunday, so he was home, a midafternoon.

"Well, there you are," Father said. "The prodigal returns."

He was a tall man, almost fifty, dark hair beginning to gray, a clear white face and pale blue eyes. He wore dark trousers and a white shirt.

"Father," I said.

He stepped out onto the small front porch, arms raised, then, suddenly, he saw Louise.

"And this is?" he asked, his hug of me arrested in midair.

"Louise," I said, "my wife."

There was a pause, then his hug, directed at me, redirected itself to her, and taking her in his long shirted arms, he said, "Of course it is."

She, little prairie flower, was nonplussed, and suffered the hug in silence, her eyes turned questioningly to me. I smiled at her, as if to say, He's like this, my father.

And then I was the victim of the hug assault.

"Come in. Come in." My father's voice brimmed with cordiality as he took the bag from Louise, then took one from me and ushered us into the house.

"Cynthia!" my father called in the hall. "Cynthia, come see your son and his bride!"

And my mother appeared at the back of the hall, coming, I would guess, from the kitchen.

She stood, in a pale green summer smock, her long brown hair down and around her shoulders, and wearing her glasses. A cautious commander, she assessed the situation, then advanced slowly. As she reached us, her weary prey, she extended her hand to Louise.

"Bride," she said.

"Ma'am," Louise said, taking my mother's hand.

"Welcome," my mother said, then to me: "Michael, you have been delinquent."

I reached down and kissed her cheek, though she never let go of Louise's hand.

My father, standing there holding suitcases, a broad grin holding his face, said, "I think what we all need is a glass of sherry."

Ah yes, the wine of family, a heady brew.

I had written my parents from Kansas, and they had written me. But my letters had been thick on form and thin on substance. I had revealed, for example, nothing of my experience at Marysville, nor had I mentioned Louise. I did tell them of McCallum's nuptials, and I had answered my mother's inquiries about my health with the vague reassurance that I was all right.

If my showing up at the homestead with a wife in tow was a surprise (and surely it was), neither my father nor my mother exhibited the least bit of shock. In fact, Louise became part and parcel of me so quickly that I suspected my parents either trusted me implicitly or simply didn't give a rat's damn. And I could not even perceive of the latter.

"She is lovely," my mother said, as she and I sat at the kitchen table drinking evening coffee.

Dad was off to the fish market, rounding up supper, and Louise was napping upstairs.

"It was a sudden thing," I said.

"Yes."

She sipped from her white cup and looked lovingly at me.

"Your wound?" she asked.

I pulled the talisman bullet from my pocket and laid it on the table.

"It fell out," I said.

She looked at the little flat-sided marble.

"No," she said.

"Yes."

She didn't touch the pellet of chaos, but she did look at it as if it were a piece of a meteor.

"Remarkable," she said.

"Quite," I said.

Mother looked at me with a quiet demeanor. "And I assume," she said, "that your Louise is the woman who shot you."

I smiled at that. "Odd, isn't it," I said, "that Cupid's arrow would be a forty-two caliber bullet."

"Odd, indeed," Mother said.

Supper was Cape Cod cod, which Louise would not touch. Catfish, perch, bass, even crawdads were acceptable to her delicate palate, but Cape Cod cod, especially in the cream sauce my mother had so lovingly prepared, was beyond my sweet darling's culinary boundaries. She ate the string beans and the mashed potatoes, but left the fish untouched.

"Louise shot Michael," Mother announced halfway through the meal.

"Did she?" my father asked.

Louise looked at the fish on her plate.

"It was, I believe, a misunderstanding," said Mother.

Louise then looked at my mother and said, "No."

"No, what, my dear?"

"It was no misunderstanding."

"Oh?"

"I did not intend," Louise said, "to be manhandled."

"Bravo," said my mother.

"Cynthia?" my father said. "Are you purposely being nasty to this child?"

"Dear me," my mother said, "I believe I am."

Louise said to my mother, "Would you like my fish?"

I ate my fish. I thought it was delicious.

After supper, my father and I sat in the backyard, smoking cigars.

"Your mother is a snapper," he said.

"So is Louise," I said.

My father took a relishing pull at his cigar, blew the smoke out in a tiny stream, then said, "They are in the kitchen alone, you know. Do you think a *rapprochement* is possible?"

"I think it is inevitable," I said.

"Fire meeting fire, so to speak."

"So to speak," I said.

It was turning evening in Providence. The murky sky had turned a pale gray-blue. In the humid air, I could smell the sea.

"Aren't women wonderful?" I said.

"God's gift," said my father.

And so they were. That night, in my old room, indeed, in my old bed, Louise and I made love so passionately that I was afraid we'd not only wake my parents but bring the house down. We were both charged with the electricity of conflict, Louise straining to make permanent her possession of me, and I straining equally to escape the clutches of my family. The lovemaking was then a kind of Magna Carta, not only a declaration of our love for each other but a ringing blow for freedom. Louise and I had bonded before, but there in the liquid hot center of nostalgia of my childhood home, we both solidified the bond and struck, too, a new and higher level of intimacy. In fact, we would later calculate that that was the night we conceived a child, an act, considering the profundity of death for all of us, of pure rebellion. A relationship that had been but passionate now became, by the simple synthesis of seed and egg, sacred.

And in the dreamy afterglow of romance spent, I thought, just before drifting away with my beloved tucked lovingly into my arms, that no matter how long I might live hence, I could never be happier than at that moment.

## III.

THE TIME IN Providence passed all too quickly. When Louise and I were not together, she was with Mother. They shopped. The education of my wild child of the prairie continued at an advanced level, and my mother proved to be an excellent tutor. Louise learned of woman things, those delicate little mysteries of which men know nothing at all.

I meanwhile read. I found that my excursion into the wild West had deprived me of books. I fell on the generous number in my mother's writing room as a hungry man would fall on a repast of long-missed foods. There was a strange and highly metaphysical novel by Melville, a gruesome collection of works by Poe, a grand novel by Dickens, dilatory works by women I did not know, and reams of *Atlantic Monthly*s. And when the home front's supply of reading material was depleted, I walked the few blocks to the Providence Public Library.

There, with the afternoon sweltering outside, I found a dark, cool corner and feasted on books, newspapers, and magazines. The world once again was a gigantic place, and the stories of that world filled a deep and empty longing in me.

It was on such an afternoon, when I was sailing the waters off Madagascar with an English reporter bound for India, that a piece of my past life drifted across my bow.

"Michael?"

I looked up from my reading chair.

"Lucinda," I said.

"My God," she said.

She walks in beauty, Byron had said, and so she still did, my former Lucinda. She wore a white summer dress, the sleeves alarmingly short, her bare, white arms in full display. Her hair was up, but still as black as midnight, and her eyes, those cold blue ices from far northern climes, were as brilliant as ever.

"You're home," she said.

"Lucinda" was all I could say.

In a dank but bright park across the way, Lucinda and I sat on the grass. It was the apex of the afternoon, and all about, Providence lay still and humid. We sat in the shade, and there was a bit of a breeze, wafting in from the sea to the south.

"You've married the whore," Lucinda said.

I looked at her with a slight frown.

"I met her," she said.

"Ah."

"She was with your mother at Schotsky's."

Schotsky's was a department store downtown.

"My mother introduced her as 'the whore'?"

"Of course not," said Lucinda. "But it was obvious."

I looked at this former love of my life with a cool disdain, then said, "There are more things in heaven and earth, Lucinda, than are dreamt of in your philosophy."

"That, my dear Michael, I am learning."

Warmth returned to my voice. "How are you, Lucinda?"

"Bereft," she said, smiling that wonderful clean smile of hers. "You are such a beast."

"Fortunate for you, then," I said, "that things turned out as they did."

She plucked a stem of grass, toyed with it a moment, then asked, "Are you happy?"

"Deliriously," I said.

"She is quite beautiful, that little tart of yours."

"And you?" I asked. "You have no prospects?"

"I am to be married in the fall."

"Oh?"

"Simon Worthington," she said.

"The Hartford Worthingtons?" I said.

"The same."

I smiled. "From worse to better."

"Indeed."

I took her hand. "My time in the West," I said, "in sometimes strenuous travails, you were my heart's delight, Lucinda. I cannot express to you properly how grateful I was, am."

"I loved you, Michael," she said, "for a while."


IV.


AND SO, in late July, Louise and I bid adieu to my parents. It had been a trip well worth taking. My father had imparted to me, in a conspiratorial moment, that my mother was much taken with my child bride. "A daughter, at last" was the way he had put it. Louise, too, I think, had found substance in our journey, a mother at last perhaps. But whatever the outcome, Louise and I returned to Washington in better circumstances than when we'd left.

The nation's capital, however, was still an oven-baked pan of beans.

Only more so.

"There's no one here," I said to Sorensen, my first day back at my duty desk.

"It's summer," said the crisp little second lieutenant. "The government shuts down."

"But the Army doesn't."

"A soldier's fate," Sorensen said. "How was your homecoming?"

"Delightful."

There was a pile of work to do. Sorensen had managed to process many of the orders, but many still remained to be dealt with. As I looked through the papers, I detected a pattern.

"More armament is going to the West," I said.

"It's a new policy," Sorensen said.

"What is a new policy?"

"'The only good Indian is a dead Indian.'"

"That is your belief?" I asked.

"General Sheridan's," he said. "I think they intend to exterminate the tribes on the plains."

"Custer's revenge."

"Actually it's Sherman's revenge," Sorensen said. "Part of a policy of total war. I think he learned it in Georgia."

I spent an hour in work, Sorensen quiet too, but as I implemented the transfers of firearms and ammunition to forts in the West, I couldn't help but feel remorseful. In my time against the Indians, I had come to respect them. They were only fighting for what was theirs. And they didn't have a chance. Uneducated men, they never understood what they were up against. Only at the Little Bighorn did they come together. With organization and the kind of leadership Crazy Horse had provided, they could have prolonged their fight indefinitely.

But I couldn't help but think that there were forces at work far greater than my meager sympathies, bigger too than Sheridan and Sherman's hot determination. Americans were not going to stay east of the Mississippi. The whole tilt of America had been to the west, and that the Caucasian population had leaped over the plains was due only to the gold in California. Now, that stampede curtailed, the railroads made mid-America not only more accessible but more desirable as well.

The time of the red man was finished. He'd had this continent for God only knows how long. At West Point, we had been taught that manifest destiny was the American destiny. I had seen such thought put into action, the encroachment on Indian lands as incessant and inevitable as the approach of a natural season. Whites could not be stopped. There were Indian leaders who knew this, and unlike Crazy Horse, they would accept the inevitable and make the best of it.

But not Crazy Horse. And he was the one Sherman would have to kill. And he was the one Sherman would kill. And when Crazy Horse was gone, the Indian nations would follow, one by one, until their great and ancient civilization was erased forever.

For a moment, there in the hot still August morning in Washington, I thought maybe I was on the wrong side. If the Indians could be organized. If they could be adequately armed. If they could only talk to one another.

"God help us if they had the telegraph," I said, more to myself than to Sorensen.

"What?"

"Nothing."

"Crofton?"

"What?"

"You're beginning to talk to yourself. That's a bad sign."

I looked at the little Michiganer and smiled. "It's the heat," I said.

"Custer was from Michigan, you know," Sorensen said.

"Land of the lunatics."

It came as no surprise a few days later that Crazy Horse had been killed. He was assassinated at Fort Robinson in Nebraska, bayoneted by an unknown trooper as he was being led to jail. He'd been tricked into coming to Fort Robinson, and once there, when he realized that he had fallen into a trap, he'd resisted.

"And was killed," I said to Sorensen, over our desks. "It's in the paper. Happened several weeks ago."

"He was the one who defeated Custer?" Sorensen asked.

"Yes."

"That should make people happy."

"The Sioux are finished now."

"*C'est la guerre,*" Sorensen said.

## V.

HE WAS beautiful.

Darien Simpson Crofton, nine pounds, four ounces, wet, shiny, his head a perfect cone from his soft-skulled passage through his mother's birth canal.

"Our baby," Louise said.

I held him as if I held all of creation.

"Here," Louise said, lifting her arms to me.

I gently placed Darien in the fold of her left arm. She took him, her face positively glowing.

"Yes," she said.

"Yes," I said, "my love."

Outside, Washington was exploding with spring.

"We'll sleep now," Louise said.

I leaned down, kissed her forehead.

Out in the hall, Sorensen smoked a huge cigar.

"She's all right?" he asked.

"Sleeping," I said.

He wore a goofy grin.

"How about a drink, Sorensen?"

"Indubitably," he said.

Across from Mercy Hospital, we found a tavern called The Angel. It was dark and cool inside, and at a little after nine in the morning, it was empty. A fat man in a white apron poured two glasses of whiskey. Sorensen and I took them to a table.

"To Darien," he said, lifting his glass.

"To Darien," I said, touching his glass.

The whiskey was hot with life.

"Damn," Sorensen said. "A baby."

"It's a miracle, Sorensen, an absolute miracle."

"Uh—Crofton?"

"What?"

"Uh—let's have another drink," Sorensen said.

"Sorensen, what is it?"

"You know, having a baby and all that, it's really great. You know, I mean . . ."

"Sorensen." My voice was a bit sharp.

"We're to go to Florida," Sorensen said.

"What?"

"Orders."

Sorensen took a folded sheet of paper out of his tunic, handed it to me. It was dated the previous day.

And there it was. Lieutenants Sorensen and Crofton were to proceed to Key West, Florida, by any available transportation. They were to make the trip unarmed and as civilians. They would check into the Trade Winds Hotel, where they would be contacted with further instructions. They must arrive in Key West on or before May 15.

"What is this?" I asked.

"I don't know."

The whiskey had lost some of its fire.

The order to Key West had been signed by a Colonel Raytheus Small. Sorensen and I found him at his home in Georgetown. It was a brilliant Sunday morning, and Colonel Small was working in his yard. A tall man in his fifties, he wore denim trousers and a dark blue work shirt. He was bald, so he wore a wide Panama hat, which he took off occasionally to wipe his sweating bald pate. He was obviously put out that Sorensen and I had tracked him to his home.

"We can deal with this tomorrow," he said, "at my office at the War Department."

"Sir," I said. "Begging the colonel's pardon, but I think it best to deal with this now."

Sorensen wore his uniform, but I was in civilian clothes, a fact that engendered in me a kind of recklessness.

Small looked menacingly at me. "Are you Sorensen?"

"No, sir, I'm Lieutenant Crofton."

"You're out of uniform, Lieutenant."

"I've been to the hospital, sir. My wife just delivered a baby."

"Oh?"

The news didn't particularly dissolve Small's irritation, but it did damage his resolve.

"The orders are clear," he said. "You and Lieutenant Sorensen are to travel to Key West by available transportation. You are to be there by the fifteenth of May. You will receive further instructions when you get there."

"Sir," I said. "I wish to protest these orders."

Small looked at me as if I had uttered an oath in a satanic tongue.

"You what?" he said.

"I am in my rights, sir," I said. "Article Fifteen of the Code of Army Conduct allows me to protest an order if I believe it compromises accepted morality."

Small stood there like a tall volcano about to let off. Then he said in a tone barely restrained, "Talk to Mr. Sorensen's father. If you continue here, I will have you arrested."

And he turned and went into his house.

After the colonel was gone, I turned to Sorensen.

"Your father?"

"That's the fly in the ointment," Sorensen said.

Our trip back to Mercy was tense. We walked. There were no horse cars running, and it was a good twenty blocks. But it was a fine day, and there was hardly anyone about.

"How did you know about that Article Fifteen?" Sorensen asked me as we walked along.

"I made it up," I said.

We walked in silence for a while, then Sorensen said, "There is no Article Fifteen?"

"There should be," I said.

I was seething, and Sorensen knew it. I was trying to restrain just a little of my anger before I lit into him about his father. Five blocks along, I thought I had regained enough composure to broach the subject.

"What," I asked Sorensen, "does your father have to do with this?"

"Well," Sorensen said, reluctant, I could tell. "He volunteered us."

"For what?"

"This mission."

I stopped. Sorensen stopped. We stood, looking at each other, eye to eye.

"What mission?" I asked.

"I don't know. I really don't."

"Why did your father volunteer us?"

"As a favor," Sorensen said, "to President Hayes."

I was, I swear to God, speechless, but I managed to spit out, "Christ!"

---

I sat with Louise and Darien the whole of the afternoon, mesmerized by their sleeping, looking at the two of them as if they were Eve and a firstborn. The entire world had just begun, and I was being sent off to God-knows-where to do God-knows-what. As I sat, my mind whirled, and I thought seriously of skedaddling. I could take Louise and the baby by way of Providence and be in Canada in three days. Once there, no one could find us.

By evening, when Louise awoke, I had determined on that course.

"Hello," she said, sleepily.

"My little prairie rose," I said, taking her hand.

She glanced down at the baby. "He's such a good baby," she said. "To sleep like this." Then she looked at me. "Do you think he's all right?"

"He's tired," I said. "He made quite a journey today."

"Yes."

"And you, my love?" I said. "How are you?"

"Sore," she said.

I stayed until a nurse made me leave, a little before nine that night. Darien woke and nursed. He loved the breast, as I did, and Louise loved giving it to him.

"My, but he sucks," she said. "He will empty me."

"Don't worry, my darling," I said. "You will replenish. You are a fountain of life."

"It's not like when you do it," she said, smiling at me.

"I do it for pleasure," I said. "He does it for supper."

"Are those mean old nurses making you go?"

"Yes."

"Will you come back?"

"Of course, first thing in the morning."

She was holding my hand, and she took it to her mouth and kissed it.

"Do you love him?" she asked.

"With all my heart."

"He is ours."

"Yes."

The Washington night was soft with stars, no moon. The air was heavy with the scent of flowers and spring. I walked slowly, feeling a myriad of emotions coursing through my mind. My whole world had changed. And then I thought of my parents. I had not told them yet. A telegram, yes, and where to send it this time of night? Union Station. So that is where I went.

Darien Simpson Crofton, 9 lbs 10 oz, born 6:58 AM, this date. Mother and child doing well.

And from Union Station, I walked to Sorensen's rooming house. It was nearly eleven when I got there, and I woke him with my knock upon his door. He let me in, wearing a nightshirt. A thin little tadpole, he looked like Jack-Be-Nimble.

"We're going to talk, Steven," I said, using his surname.

Sorensen's room was smallish, table, chairs, bed, chamber pot. He went back to bed, lay down, head on his pillow, drawing the covers up. I dragged a chair over to his bed.

"I'm not going," I said.

He cocked open an eye at that.

I went on. "I'm taking Louise and the baby to Canada."

Sorensen cocked open a second eye at that, then said, "All right. Do you need any money?"

"No."

"Good luck," he said, and shut his eyes.

The little tadpole went to sleep.

I sat there a long while. A little after midnight, I too dropped off to sleep.

———

"You yourself told me," I said. "You've never even fired a gun."

"That's true," Sorensen said.

"Yet we're being sent south, to Cuba I figure, where there has been fighting for ten years."

"It wasn't my idea."

We sat at Sorensen's small table, drinking some atrocious coffee. It was just gray daylight outside. He still wore his nightshirt.

"Why in God's name would your father volunteer you for something like that?"

"I don't know," Sorensen said. "I suspect he thinks it will make a man out of me."

"A dead man."

Sorensen didn't say anything to that.

"And why me?" I asked. "Your father doesn't even know me."

Sorensen, looking a little sheepish, said softly, "I asked for you."

"What?"

"Well, Jesus, Crofton, what do I know about anything? You've been out there shooting Indians. If we are to go to Cuba, I thought you might know something about shooting Cubans."

"You asked for me?"

"Well, who else was I going to ask for? Napoleon? That fool knows how to clean a pistol, not shoot one."

"You asked for me?"

"Dad thought it was a good idea. He pulled your record. Did you shoot a bunch of Klansmen out in Kansas? It wasn't in your record, but he heard a story."

"You knew Louise was about to birth a baby."

"Yeah."

"I'm a father now."

Sorensen looked forlornly at his coffee cup. "I'll help you get to Canada," he said.

"Shit!"

I could have killed Sorensen. I left his dilapidated little room before I did kill him. But not before I drew out of him a few more details about the mysterious mission.

Sorensen's father, the Congressman, sat on a committee of Latin American affairs. He, and others whom Congressman Sorensen would not name, even to his son, had been involved in brokering a peace between warring factions in Cuba. These men had come up with a delicate plan concerning that brokered peace. Sorensen and I were to be a part of that plan. As to what part, Steven did not know, and his father had told him only that it would be explained once Steven and I arrived in Key West.

Congressman Sorensen did say that President Hayes had approved the plan. Further, the President was pleased that the Congressman had volunteered his son. As his father had put it to Steven, "It will be a real feather in both our caps."

"And did your father say it would be dangerous?"

Sorensen got a squeamish look on his face, but he said nothing.

"Sorensen."

He looked at me, a soft pleading in his eyes. "My father said there was a chance we'd be killed."

I felt a dry surge of disgust, rising like the bile of nausea. "It's Cuba," I said. "And it's something dirty."

Canada—the great north, uncluttered, clean, and cold.

Just before I left Sorensen, I asked him, "If I don't go with you, will you still go?"

He didn't really want to answer. He didn't at all like his answer. And I swear there was a tear in his eye when he said, "Yes."

All the way to Mercy Hospital, I thought to myself, I'm not Sorensen's keeper. I already have a child.

"You must not go," Louise said.

I'd told her the whole thing, violating probably a dozen Army regulations. It was early at Mercy, a half hour before visiting hours. I'd been so strenuous with the nurse on duty, she could not refuse me.

Little Darien slept, on his mother's bosom.

"I know that," I said.

"We just had a baby," Louise said. "Don't they know that?"

"I will talk to someone," I said.

She lay on her back, and she looked away from me. I was holding her hand.

Turning back to me, she said, "Why did Steven do this? Why did he do this?"

"He had no choice," I said.

"God," she said, and Louise never took the Lord's name in vain.

I hadn't mentioned the Canada plan to Louise. And I had been purposely vague when I'd said I would talk to someone. There really wasn't anyone to talk to. Orders were orders, and with a Congressman and the President involved, I would get no reprieve from any ranking officers.

And there it was, a classic double bind. For six years, I had devoted myself not only to the Army but to the notion of the Army: duty, honor, country. Ours not to reason why. If there was one thing that had been hammered home at West Point, it was the absolute moral necessity of obedience. An army without obedience was an army without discipline, and an army without discipline was an army defeated. I had been ordered to Key West—not asked to go, ordered. To disobey the order was to be a criminal.

Yet I had a duty too to my family, to my wife, to my son. Was that duty not sacrosanct also? There was a higher law involved here. No doubt Louise and Darien would survive my absence, but would I? And what but some malignant force of the universe could take me away at a time like this?

But my choices were severely limited. In fact, there were but two: obey or not obey. To not obey meant to become a fugitive, with a wife and child in tow. Canada, the ice and cold of dereliction and shame.

"Take me to Providence," Louise said. "Darien and me."

"What?"

"We'll stay with your parents while you are gone."

"Louise."

She looked at me, that straight, business look in her eyes.

"You have to go," she said. "Because of Steven."

"He might well die if I do."

"Both of you might," she said, gripping my hand ferociously, as tears streamed down her face.


## VI.


AND SO, a bright morning in May, our little entourage boarded a train in Union Station bound for the north. It was a somber ride. Even Darien seemed subdued. He hardly fussed at all. Sorensen was the other child on the trip. He was acutely morose, sitting against the car's window, a look of abject pity glued to his face. His despair wasn't so much the result of his trip into danger as his self-inflicted shame at dragging me along. He could not look at Louise, which was just as well, as her disgust with him was easily registered. Rightly or wrongly, she put the horrid responsibility of this whole mess on the little tadpole from Michigan. She did not speak to him, not a single word, the whole way.

Sorensen made the trip to Providence only because I had arranged, through my father, for passage from there to Key West via a packet bound for Vera Cruz. The ship, the *Semper Fidelis,* was a contract vessel out of Providence, captained by a man named Augustus Flogg, that made regular trade runs down the East Coast and into the Gulf of Mexico. At times it shipped my father's harness merchandise, and it was due to depart Providence on May 7. Flogg had told my father that he could deliver Sorensen and me to Key West by May 14 or so.

A flurry of telegrams between my parents and me had so far been the cost of the expedition. I could tell which of the telegrams from Providence had been dictated by my mother and which had been of my father's origin. Hers were negative in the extreme, while his were noted for their resignation. But in three short, hectic days, we had put together the logistics of the situation, an organizational accomplishment to make any military man proud.

The only positive among the sea of negatives was Darien. He proved to be a great little trooper, and underneath all of his grandmother's bristling disapproval, there was her purely selfish desire to put her hands upon the seed of her seed. Two or three of all her telegrams asked about the boy. Though she made no effort to disguise it, she could not have hidden her joy at the prospect of holding this magnificent child.

"Louise?"

"Yes?"

Just north of New York, the sun down, night coming, I leaned against my wife, who held Darien, and I asked her, "Do you still have that derringer?"

"Yes."

"I'll be taking it with me."

"Of course," she said.

———

Providence was a whirl. My father and mother met us at the station with a four-by pulled by a team of two. We all piled into the carriage, and had Jesus Christ Himself been with us, He would not have received the attention that Darien Simpson Crofton received. His grandmother cried when she first held him, fat tears of ownership coursing down her cheeks. My father, driving, could only repeat again and again, "Remarkable. Remarkable." Louise and I sat, proud parents, in the back of the carriage, embellished, no doubt, with the same feelings a rapacious Spaniard had felt when laying a treasure at the feet of Ferdinand and Isabella.

There would be no sleep, except for Darien. We had arrived the night before the sailing of the *Semper Fidelis,* and the time before the tide was spent drinking, first, a delicious port my father had acquired at Nantucket, then coffee into the wee hours before dawn.

Sorensen, caught up in the festivity of family, lost a bit of his gloominess; but the star attraction, even in his sleep, was the baby boy Darien. He slept in a crib in the bedroom just off the kitchen, in my crib in fact, pulled down from the attic for this special occasion. Mother and Louise kept making expeditions into the bedroom to stare with wonder upon the sleeping child.

My father, knowing of course that Sorensen and I were bound for Key West, had guessed that our final destination was Cuba, and he elaborated upon the political conditions there, having followed the story of those conditions regularly in the Boston papers.

The peace between the rebels and the Spanish was, according to my father, a patchwork thing. The war, and it was a war in every sense of the word, had been going on for ten years, but neither side had gained an advantage. The peace agreement, called the Pact of Zanjon, would not hold, my father said. Not all the rebels had agreed to it.

My father's final say on the matter was "The U.S.

intends to annex Cuba, one way or another. That is our sole interest. The Spanish know this, as do the rebels. We are but spectators at a dogfight. It doesn't really matter which dog wins, because the winner will, eventually, answer to us."

Then it was the time of departure, a heavy affair, our lack of sleep stiffened by apprehension.

My mother, in her farewell embrace, whispered to me, "Come back, my darling. Come back to your son, to your wife, to me."

And Louise, surreptitiously slipping me her near-deadly little derringer, also whispered, "If they try to take your life, kill them any way you can."

Blonde and blue-eyed, my wife, nonetheless, was an Apache, and I loved her dearly.

I held the sleeping Darien, alone in the bedroom, held him against my breast, and I breathed in his powerful smell and ran my hand slowly over his silken head. I loved his mother, dearly, but the love I felt at that moment for that boy was as powerful a love as I had ever felt, or ever would.

At dockside, my father said, "Don't worry about Louise or your child."

"I won't," I said.

Dawn was creaking across the water of Providence Harbor.

An embrace, my father a long-armed man, his arms all the way around me.

"Caution," he whispered.

"I love you, Father."

"And I you, my son."

And then Sorensen and I were shipboard, bound for the south.

———

The big Navy Colt fairly flew out of Sorensen's hand when it discharged. I grabbed it before it hit the deck floor.

"Jesus," he said.

"You can't be dropping it like that, Sorensen," I said.

We stood at the rail on the port side of the *Semper Fidelis*. We were a day out of Providence, somewhere off the coast of Delaware. I was giving Sorensen shooting lessons with a pistol I had borrowed from Captain Flogg. It was early morning and the sea was calm. The Atlantic Ocean was in no great danger, because I was fairly certain that Sorensen couldn't hit it.

Sorensen asked, "Does it always, you know, explode like that?"

"It's an older gun, an older model," I said, "but yes, it does always explode like that. It's in the grip, *amigo*. You hold the butt firmly, but your finger should be light on the trigger."

I placed the gun again in Sorensen's hand.

"Use two hands," I said. "Your right hand around the butt, and your left hand around that hand. There. Yes. Now extend your arms, lock your elbows. Steady now.

Sight along the barrel. Pick a wave. Put that front sight on the wave. Then squeeze the trigger, slowly."

BAM!

A hundred feet out, the bullet raised a spout of water three feet high. Sorensen hadn't dropped the gun this time.

"Well," he said, still holding the gun with his arms extended. "That's keen."

"You hit the ocean, Sorensen. Hell of a shot."

We finished our firing exercise after twelve shots. Sorensen had managed to hold the pistol on eleven. That was, I sorely believed, about the extent of his skill as a marksman.

Above deck, I returned the pistol to Captain Flogg after cleaning it. He stood at the helm, the ship's great wheel in each of his hands.

"Thank you, Captain," I said, laying the big Colt on a table at the rear of the cabin.

"Key West is a rich one," he said, in a low, rumbling voice. Decades at sea had given his voice a salty flavor. "Mostly wreckers and *cigaristas.*"

"I doubt we'll be there long," I said.

"Aye. It's Cuba, I'd think. A very dangerous place."

"You've been there?"

"I've done favors," Flogg said.

The ship, a steamer but wholly under sail at the moment, plowed south through the green water.

"Lad?"

"Sir?"

"Do you have religion?"

"Yes, sir, I do."

"I'd set about my prayers, were I you."

"Aye," I said.

In the cabin that Sorensen and I shared, the little *pistolero* was asleep on his bunk. I lay down on mine. The gentle roll of the ship was comforting, and there was only the sound of the bow slapping against the water.

I pulled from my pants pocket Louise's derringer. It was an older model, twin-barreled, side by side, like a small shotgun. There were two hammers but only one trigger, a double-action, half a pull for the left barrel, another half a pull for the right. I unloaded the gun.

Two balls, forty-two centimeters in diameter, and two powder loads, small packages in wax paper to fit behind the balls. There was a small ramrod fitted beneath the two barrels. Tiny percussion caps fitted in the holes below the two hammers. It was a complicated weapon, but its design was functional. I could, of course, not know truly if the powder packets would still work—or the percussion caps, for that matter. And with only two shots, I could not waste either to test.

I reloaded the weapon, made sure the hammers were down in a safe position, and slipped it back into my pocket.

There were stops, at Baltimore, again at Hampton Roads, and Charleston. The *Semper Fidelis* off-loaded and on-loaded. A crew of four was busy arranging and rearranging cargo. In port, if there was time, Sorensen and I went ashore. The farther south we got, the hotter it got; and in Charleston, the War of the Rebellion seemed not over at all. Confederate flags flew from several buildings, and there were men in gray everywhere, not soldiers, but not exactly civilians either. Many, I noticed, were without limbs. And their speech, when I heard it, was like none I'd ever heard before. It was English, but lazy and fluid, humid like the heavy, hot air itself.

"God," Sorensen muttered, as we walked a street near the harbor in Charleston, "there are Rebs everywhere."

"Ruins, too," I said. "Look at the burned buildings."

"Sherman," Sorensen said.

"I think it most fortunate," I said, "that we are not in uniform."

"Amen," Sorensen said.

We were glad to be back aboard the *Semper Fidelis* and glad, too, to sail away from Charleston. At sea, ten miles off the coast, the air was sweeter and the sense of safety as sweet.

In port at Savannah, Sorensen and I didn't leave the ship.

Off the east coast of Florida, Sorensen and I sat on the cargo hold at the back of the ship. There was no wind. Flogg had resorted to steam power, and the wheel at the stern turned relentlessly, the engine driving it making a steady clatter beneath us.

It was unmercifully hot, even out at sea.

Sorensen asked me, "Do you think Cuba will be like this? This hot?"

"No doubt," I said.

"This is like D.C., only outside."

"Baked *frijoles*," I said.

We could see the coastline, a mere ten miles away off the starboard side. The sea was flat and calm to the shore, but there were rising wrinkles of heat once the water touched the land.

"You know, Crofton, I don't really want to do this."

"Why, Steven, it's an adventure."

"My father," Sorensen said, "he's . . ."

I waited for him to finish the sentence, but he didn't. There was a long silence, and I glanced at the little tadpole. He was staring at Florida, his face darker now from the sun.

"Why did you ever join the army, Sorensen?"

"For the women," he said.

"For the women?"

"I thought the uniform would attract them."

"Has it?"

"Only the ones that I've paid, down at Dolly's on F Street."

"What about your father?" I asked.

"He's a fool," said Sorensen. "An opportunistic, butt-kissing fool."

I smiled. "Must be an excellent politician."

"He's that," said Sorensen.

## VII.

"MY GOD, it's Cuba," Sorensen said.

And it certainly didn't look like America. Key West was a teeming metropolis, filled with Latins. Before dropping us off, Flogg had told us that the ten-year fight in Cuba had forced thousands of rebel sympathizers to Key West, many of them revolutionaries escaped to the Florida Keys to avoid capture by the Spaniards. They had brought with them tobacco, more particularly cigars, and the city now boasted hundreds of "confectionaries," tobacco shops plying the products of the cigar factories located in the western half of the city.

Sorensen and I stood on the dock, a couple of castups, a carpetbag each, our trousers, waistcoats, and low-brimmed hats not at all suited to the thick, hot atmosphere that reeked with a thousand smells, each borne on a fetid, humid air as thick as butter.

I think that I had expected a sleepy little island town with beaches and swaying palm trees, but what I got instead was a bustling city, vibrant with energy and opportunity. Key West was rich with paved streets and tall buildings and fine homes. And dockside was the heart, liver, and lungs of the town: scores of boats, teams of laborers, and fat horses straining at wagonloads of cargo.

We heard hundreds of voices, each and every one of them speaking Spanish.

"Sorensen?" I said.

"What?"

"Do you speak Spanish?"

"No, do you?"

"*Un poco.*"

"Well, let's *un poco* up into town," he said. "We look like a couple of Ichabods standing out here."

After about an hour, a late-morning hour, with the streets alive with crowds, and not daring to ask directions, we found the Trade Winds Hotel. It was a two-story building tucked in between an immense cantina/saloon and a post office flying, incongruously, the American flag. The lobby of the hotel was spacious and cool and crowded, too, with well-dressed men smoking cigars and speaking their singsong language in rapid bursts.

A room was a problem. There didn't seem to be any, until I laid a $20 gold piece on the counter. The desk clerk, a thin, imperial fellow with a high and stiff collar, smiled graciously, and the gold piece disappeared as quick as lightning. A large, leather registry was swiveled around, a pen was proffered, and I signed: Mr. Smith and Mr. Jones, from Kansas USA.

Several boys appeared out of nowhere, anxious to relieve Sorensen and me of our small traveling bags, but we deferred. Key in hand, we mounted stairs at the back of the lobby, ascended to the second floor, found Room No. 21, and settled in.

There were two beds, against opposite walls, a washstand, desk, chair, and floor-to-ceiling windows, open to the sounds and songs of the street outside. Sorensen sat ceremoniously on the bed against the east wall, and I sat on the bed opposite. We both sat there, a couple of strangers in a very strange land, and looked at each other.

Finally, Sorensen spoke. "What now?"

"We wait," I said.

Sorensen agreed that we should stick to the room. But about sundown, he went in search of supper. He returned an hour later with food and beer. The food was two bowls made of bread, filled with a spicy combination of rice, beans, chicken, peppers, and small, succulent shrimp. The beer was cold.

"It's cold," I said, fondling the brown bottle with the cork and wire top.

"Ice," he said.

I looked, askingly.

"Next door," Sorensen said. "Wonderful place, big, airy, cool. They got ice in a big box at the back. All the drinks are cold."

I tasted the rice mixture. Delicious. "What is this?"

"Food."

And the beer, it was ambrosia.

We ate in silence, each of us dedicated to the task at hand. When the course was finished, we ate the bowls, the bread soaked with the residue of the splendid rice-and-bean concoction. The last of the beer had not lost its cooling.

"There," I said, leaning back on my bed. "That was something."

Sorensen pulled two cigars from his shirt pocket, tossed me one. A packet of matches, he lit his, tossed the packet to me.

Blowing out a blue stream of smoke, he said, "We are in cigar heaven, *amigo.*"

And indeed we were.

A bit later, fine Cuban tobacco layered atop fine Cuban cooking, Sorensen gave me some background to Key West.

"I found out what a wrecker is," he said. "They're the guys who salvage the ships. Dangerous reefs all about. Ships go aground, these wrecker fellows go out and pick the vessel clean. Get to keep whatever they find. Some kind of law."

"And you found this out how?"

"The bartender next door, Irish fellow. Fine gentleman, from Boston. The Americans are the wreckers. The Cubans are the *cigaristas.* Everybody's happy."

"And what did you tell the Irish bartender of yourself?"

"That I'm a Kansas cattleman."

"Plenty of cattle here," I said.

"These fellows are partial to beefsteaks," Sorensen said. "The Irishman told me they get their meat from up-key, wherever that is." He took another draw on his cigar. "You know, that's not a bad idea. Get some Texas cattle, put them on a boat, sail them over. Lots of money here."

"Guns would be better," I said.

And thus our first night in Key West. It cooled a bit when the sun was down. We left our big windows open. The town didn't even attempt sleep until well after midnight.

The morning was even better, quiet, cool, a smell of the rain that had passed through briefly before sunrise.

As Sorensen slept, I stood at the windows, wearing only my trousers. The street below was relatively empty, just a few passersby, and above the buildings I could see a low ridge of golden clouds. The water wasn't visible, but I could smell it. That smell, and the smell of the fresh rain, washed away the fetid, hot odor of the night before.

We had arrived on our target date, the fifteenth. I had no idea what was to happen now, only that we were to be contacted by someone. Our trip, our location, the lazy, tropical morning, all took a distant place in my mind, for at the front were sweet thoughts of Louise and Darien. As I stood at the big window, I seemed to be with them, their smells and feels a part of me, and for an instant I felt such a deep and abiding longing that I almost cried. I actually could feel the tears welling up behind my hungry eyes. And I probably would have thought myself into a torrent of salty water had I not been disturbed by a light knock at the door.

I moved across the room, slapping Sorensen's foot but gesturing for him to be quiet as he opened his eyes. Then, Louise's derringer still in my pocket but my right hand cocking the two hammers, I leaned against the door.

"Yes?" I said.

From the other side, a soft voice: "Mr. Jones? Smith?"

"Who are you?"

"A friend."

"What do you want?"

"Talk."

"Are you armed?" I asked.

"Of course."

I looked at Sorensen. He slipped out of his bed, wearing only his undershorts, and assumed a position the other side of me beside the door. I undid the latch, turned the knob, and slowly opened the door. I peeked around it, and there stood a white man, dressed conspicuously like a Cuban, white pants, a dingy white pullover shirt, and a straw field hat. He appeared to be in his late twenties, and he had a large bag on a tote over his right shoulder. He wore an immense grin.

"B. Jordan Humphries," he said, "of Syracuse, New York."

Inside the room, the door once more latched, Humphries said, "Sorensen and Crofton, I assume." And he extended his hand to both of us, shaking each in turn. "Welcome to Key West. Lovely, isn't it?"

I asked, "What are we to do, Humphries?"

"Take guns to the rebels," he said. "We'll go tonight."

Sorensen asked, "Are you in the Army?"

Humphries thought a bit before answering, "Well, not exactly. I believe I could be considered a private contractor."

"You run guns," I said.

"Among other things." He pulled the strap off his shoulder, held up the bag, which appeared heavy, and gestured with it toward my bed. "May I?"

I nodded.

Humphries set the bag on the bed, pulled open the drawstring, reached inside, and fished out two pistols. Handing one to me, the other to Sorensen, he said, "Colts. Model 1878. Double action, forty-five caliber, seven-and-a-half-inch barrels. Brand new. This is the cutting edge, gentlemen. Not a finer pistol in the world."

"You're a salesman?" Sorensen said.

"In a manner of speaking," Humphries said.

"What are we to do with these?" I asked.

"Nothing, I hope," Humphries said. "They are for your personal protection. But we have a hundred more to deliver to Antonio Maceo, one of the rebels. He's at the eastern end of the island with an army, or what's left of an army."

"Ammunition?" I said.

"A thousand cartridges," Humphries said. And reaching again into his bag, he brought out two boxes of bullets and handed one each to Sorensen and me.

Sorensen asked, "How are we to get to Cuba?"

"I have a boat."

The gun was heavy in my hand.

Sorensen said, "I've never been to Syracuse."

"Wonderful town," Humphries said. "And the university, ah, they have the best baseball team in the conference."

"What do you know of all this?" I asked.

"All of what?" he asked.

"This expedition, the guns, this fellow Maceo."

Once again Humphries reached into his bag. He withdrew a bottle of rum, a full bottle.

"Let's speak as gentlemen in a great cause," he said, uncorking the bottle.

And through the morning, with a taste of rum now and then as a stimulant, we learned of the history of a revolution. Humphries tutored us in the shadings, mostly gray, of the grisly affair.

The revolution had begun in Cuba in 1868, a local affair, at some sugarcane plantation, but it had quickly spread. The Cubans wanted to be free of the Spanish, but the Spanish, already having lost an empire in the New World, were determined not to lose Cuba, their "pearl of the Antilles," as Humphries put it.

The war had gone on and on, neither side able to claim victory, and it had turned, sadly, into a conflict of attrition. There were horrendous casualties, mostly civilians, and barbaric acts on both sides. Antonio Maceo had emerged as the finest rebel, certainly the most successful. "He is a tiger," Humphries said.

"He defeated superior Spanish forces in a half-dozen conflicts," Humphries said. "Just last February, outnumbered eight to one, with only about forty men, he fought for three hours, routed a Spanish troop of three hundred. He is cunning, he is forceful, and he is unbelievably brave.

"The Spanish offered him a fortune to accept the Pact of Zanjon. He refused. He is a patriot. All the other rebel leaders, they want to quit. But not Maceo. He intends to fight the Spanish bastards until they leave the island."

"And now," Sorensen said, "we are taking these new Colt pistols to him."

"Indeed," Humphries said, taking a swig from the rum bottle.

"Humphries?" I said.

He looked at me.

I then said, "You don't need us to take pistols to the rebels. You could do that on your own."

"Ah, true, my friend. May I ask, are you college educated?"

"West Point, class of seventy-four."

"I'm Yale myself," he said, "class of 'seventy-two."

"Why are Sorensen and I here?"

"You are to kill Maceo."


## VIII.


I DIDN'T cotton to the idea of assassination. Maceo wasn't an enemy of the United States—at least I didn't see how he was. Yet there was an order to kill him. I thought of my imaginary Article 15, the imagined right of a soldier to refuse to obey an immoral order, but I thought, too, of the repercussions of disobeying an order. But I didn't know, I honestly didn't know, if I could do this, to kill a man in cold blood, simply because somebody, somewhere high up, wanted him dead.

The run from Key West to Baracoa at the eastern tip of the large island of Cuba would take a good bit of the afternoon and all of the night. Humphries's boat was a sponger, a small craft, no more than thirty feet long, with a small steam motor and a screw propeller. A small cabin sat in the middle of the boat, the wheelhouse; and our cargo, two wooden crates under canvas, was lashed down astern to put the propeller deeper into the water.

Sorensen and I sat, our backs to the front wall of the wheelhouse, Humphries above us, guiding the craft. It was evening, the sun playing upon the water, which was a grand green and turquoise in color, but flat, hardly any chop. The boat bumped along on a south-by-southeast course.

Sorensen and I both were plagued by a strange reluctance, a doubt that gnawed at us like church mice at work on the Eucharist bread.

We were being sent to kill a man. That alone was a devilish task, enough to erode whatever virtue we might claim. But to make a bad matter worse, the man we were to kill did not, as far as we could determine, deserve it.

Back in the hotel room, before we left on our deadly mission, Sorensen had voiced his concern. He had asked Humphries, point-blank, why. Why kill Maceo? He was a hero. And didn't we, the United States, support him, his movement, the idea of a free Cuba? If we were taking guns to Maceo, that must indicate some kind of allegiance. Assassination seemed contrary to all we, the good old U.S. of A., stood for.

Why were we to kill Maceo?

Humphries's answer had been succinct and spoke volumes.

"Sugar," he said.

The boat pushed on, the sea calm. There was just a faint darkening to the sky in the east.

Sorensen said, "This is a fool's errand."

I said nothing. Instead, I pulled the pistol from my waist. It was a good gun. Humphries was right about that. I'd loaded it before we checked out of the Trade Winds, the .45 cartridges squat and fat, likely to do a lot of damage to whoever was hit by one. The seven-and-a-half-inch barrel gave the gun some distance, a hundred feet maybe. After that, hitting a target would be mostly luck.

Back at the hotel, I had asked Humphries, "The Spaniards have been trying to kill this Maceo fellow for ten years. If they can't do it, what makes anyone think Sorensen and I can? We're just a couple of clerks."

"You can get close," Humphries said. "He'll trust you. You're bringing him weapons."

"The pistols are bait."

"Precisely."

I asked, "And after we shoot him, what do we do?"

"Run," Humphries had said.

I cocked and uncocked the pistol. It had a smooth, fast action.

"Sorensen?"

"What?"

"You won't have to cock it to fire it. Just pull the trigger. It cocks itself."

The boat was moving at about five knots. The breeze in our faces was cool and fresh.

Sorensen asked, "Why do they want Maceo dead?"

"He burns cane fields," I said.

"So?"

"That drives up the price of sugar."

Sorensen was quiet awhile, then he muttered, "Jesus."

And I could tell Sorensen was having the same problem I was having.

The darkness came quickly once the sun was down. Soon we were running with just starlight.

———

I spelled Humphries at the wheel. Sorensen and I would take two-hour shifts driving the boat until about an hour before dawn, when Humphries said we'd be near Baracoa. The engine for the small boat was below the wheelhouse, its boiler fed with coal, a hamper of which was also in the wheelhouse. All that was required was to drop a lump into the feed chute when the steam pressure reached a certain number on the dial mounted next to the wheel. The little steam engine was not too loud, and Humphries instructed Sorensen and me on navigating. We simply had to follow a star, keeping it on the bow, and by the time it had passed behind us with the spin of the earth, Humphries would be awake to find another.

We were to put in at a cove west of Baracoa, an isolated spot Humphries had used before. The plan, if it could be called that, was to reach our destination before dawn, put our small boat and its deadly cargo into the cove, hide it as well as we could, and wait. The rebels were to meet us there. Exactly how Sorensen and I would go about our lethal business was not known—indeed, it could not be planned. It would be based simply on opportunity. But two things were certain: The rebels would not get the guns, and Humphries would provide Sorensen and me our means of escape.

It all seemed so dreadfully simple. Sorensen and I would shoot and kill a hero of the revolution, then sail leisurely back to Key West. It all seemed so simple that I was absolutely sure it wouldn't work. I knew, going in, that were Sorensen and I even able to get a shot off at our prey, his retainers would gun us down on the beach. As for Humphries, I wasn't at all sure that he wouldn't put us ashore, then abscond, leaving my compadre and me to whatever fate was in store for us.

"Oh," Humphries said before turning in on a blanket at the bow of the boat, "there are also the Spanish. They have patrol boats in the waters around Baracoa. They don't own the land down there, but they do own the water."

"Humphries?" I said.

"Yes?"

"This is a botch, all the way."

In the dim light of the cabin, I could see his mischievous smile.

"But grand fun, don't you think, sport?"

And then I was alone with the vessel, the sea, and the star to guide us.

———

Behind us all was a verdant green, lush and deep. There was not a breath of wind. Sweat dripped off our faces like water from a spigot. The quiet was so heavy as actually to be felt, like a hot and bright blanket thrown over us. Sorensen and I sat on the bow of the boat. Humphries sat at the stern. We had our pistols out, but I didn't know what good they would have done us. The vessel was pushed in against a wall of jungle. Someone could have reached out and tapped us on the shoulder before we would even know he was there. We had cut limbs and brush to hide us from the port side.

To the east there was a curving shore and a sand beach, but the beach was narrow, backed by another wall of jungle. All we could actually see clearly was water, the small glassy bay that came to a point a half mile opposite us. It was only an hour after dawn, but already the heat was unmerciful, and insects were about, snapping at us with buzz and bite.

"Yellow fever," Sorensen whispered.

"What?"

"A real killer. Dead in twenty-four hours."

"Sorensen?"

"Yeah?"

"Shut up."

There we sat, three pilgrims in a cathedral of green.

We had water, a three-gallon tin, which tinted the warm drink. And we had food, crackers and sardines, purely epicurean. A nice white wine would have turned the occasion into a picnic.

It was almost impossible to stay awake. The heat was a narcotic. Every ten minutes or so my head would drop, and my chin touching my chest would wake me, that or the sweat stinging my eyeballs. Reaching over the rail of the boat, I brought a handful of water up to drench my face. I could taste the salt, which only made me thirsty.

"There's this one," Sorensen said. "Ida Mae."

Sorensen's voice was hushed.

"Crofton? You would not believe her ass. White as snow and the size of New Hampshire. I mean, it is a wonder of nature. She's tiny. Small feet, miniature fingers, exquisite features, but that ass. The earth bulging below the equator."

I looked at Sorensen. He had a truly dreamy stare.

"Three dollars," he said to the waters of the bay. "Hardly anyone asks for her. Dolly told me that I'd saved the girl her employment." Sorensen turned to look at me. "That ass alone is worth three dollars," he said in all seriousness. "Smooth as rubber. And white, oh my. The Moby Dick of asses."

"Sorensen," I said. "You are a very strange person."

We waited through the morning, into the afternoon. There was nothing astir. Even the birds were quiet. By evening, Humphries was growing philosophical.

"Cuban time," he said. He'd joined Sorensen and me at the bow. "A different concept altogether. I think it has something to do with the climate. Have you noticed it? The farther north one gets, the more acute becomes our awareness of time. Down south, it hardly matters."

"What if they don't come?" Sorensen asked.

"Well, then," Humphries said. "We've had ourselves a relaxing little voyage, got away from the stress and strain of the city. Not altogether a waste. Eh?"

I asked Humphries, "How long have you been at this?"

"Let's see," he said, "I came down in seventy-three, had a nice little arrangement with both sides. Odd, isn't it, the money to be made in a war? There was thought then that the rebels would win. I've been in and out, five years, seems longer."

"And you speak Spanish," I said.

"As one of the natives."

"What did you study at Yale?"

He looked at me and smiled. "Theology," he said. "Curious, you know, about how the Divinity plays in this world."

"How does it?" I asked.

"Doesn't, old man. Darwin is right. We're just a bunch of monkeys."

"With Colt pistols."

"Sad, isn't it?" he said.

The night came. Again, we divided the night, two-hour shifts. We took kerosene from the lamp in the wheelhouse and rubbed it on our hands and faces to ward off the mosquitoes. But still the night was miserable. The heat didn't seem to abate at all, and I thought, What a hellish place to fight a war. There was an hour, before dawn, that it was cool enough to sleep.

A sip of tinnish water, a few sardines and musty crackers, and another sip of warm water, our breakfast complete.

"Is this what war is like?" Sorensen asked me.

"Pretty much," I said.

"Food is lousy, too," he said.

## IX.

"I'M GOING DOWN to Baracoa," Humphries said. "I'll hike it. Anybody shows up, you boys stall till I get back. Shouldn't take long."

And he was off, walking along the bloody beach like a tourist.

"Some fellow," Sorensen said, watching him.

"You think he's from Syracuse?" I asked.

"I think he's from Mars," Sorensen said.

Humphries didn't come back, not that day. Sorensen and I stayed as awake as we could, but the lack of sleep in the hot night caught up with both of us, and we took turns napping. The day was a duplicate of the last, still and hot, though there was a storm to the east toward evening. We could see the clouds, high and bright, then streaks of jagged lightning. But it missed us and didn't even send a breeze. By night, both Sorensen and I were beginning to fade.

Sorensen drew the final two hours of the night, and after he relieved me, I lay down on the boat deck and felt the final cooling of the night. It came as pure nourishment to my sleepy soul. And it seemed I had just drifted blessedly off when Sorensen woke me.

"Spaniards," he whispered.

Every nerve in my body tightened.

It was a patrol boat, just rounding the far point of our bay. The Spanish flag was clearly visible on the stern. Two men with rifles stood at the bow, and at the stern, another, with binoculars.

They chugged along slowly, not two hundred yards offshore.

Our boat was pulled in close to the jungle shore, and we rested under a canopy of trees. We'd cut branches and laid them over our port side, along with brush. I thought, They will have to be looking exactly for us to see us. But, I also thought, maybe they were. Humphries, maybe they've taken him.

"What do we do?" Sorensen asked, his voice raspy with fear.

"We don't move," I said. "Stay stock-still."

"And if they come in?"

"We fight them," I said.

Closer the Spanish boat drew, across the mouth of our small bay. The soldiers were clearly visible now. They wore what looked like Panama hats, and they had bandoleers of ammunition across their chests. The man at the back with the binoculars was an officer, I could tell. There was a cabin in the middle of the boat, a wheelhouse, one man inside. Four of them. Two rifles. The man in the wheelhouse probably had a rifle, too. I could just make out the rifles: bolt action, repeaters. If they could see us, they could hit us.

Sorensen and I lay sprawled behind the rail of the boat in front of the pilothouse. Just our eyes were above the rail. I didn't think the wood planking would stop a rifle bullet. But at least we were out of sight. If they did see the boat, they might think it was empty. That would get them close enough so our pistols might have some effect.

They drew closer, closer, then were directly abreast of our stern. If they were to see us, I thought, it would be now.

And then they were gone, on past, out of our sight. I could hear the engine, moving away.

"Jesus," Sorensen muttered, and for the first time since I'd heard him use the word, it sounded like a prayer.

Fear woke us up. Bodies that had been mired in the mud of heat and exhaustion were suddenly revived. It was as if a jolt of electricity had been sent coursing through us, and now, animated by sheer terror, we were as alert as animals.

"Do you think they saw us?" Sorensen asked. "They would have stopped if they saw us. Wouldn't they?"

We were poised now, at the stern, knelt down behind the canvas over our damning cargo.

"Hush," I said.

I listened intently, but I could hear nothing, not the engine of the Spanish boat, for which I listened particularly. There was only the sound of the water slipping ashore, and the usual noise of the bush.

After ten minutes, with Sorensen leaning against the cargo, pistol in hand, and I too, gun at ready, both of us breathing rapidly but as quiet as we could, I said, "All right."

"God," Sorensen muttered. "I was scared out of my mind."

I looked at him and grinned. "Cleans away the muck, doesn't it?"

"What would we have done?" he asked. "I mean, there were four of them."

"With rifles," I added.

"Crofton?"

"What?"

"When Louise shot you?"

"Yeah?"

"What was it like?"

"It hurt," I said.

Humphries's absence now grated on us, like a rock rubbed across a wound. Our instincts were to take flight. The waiting, the uncertainty of his return, only goaded that instinct, and by the noon hour, Sorensen gave it voice.

"I think we should pull out of here," he said.

"Without Humphries?"

"He might not be coming back. He might be dead."

We were sitting again at the front of the boat. The doldrums of the heat and the boredom had returned. We hadn't eaten, and had had only a few sips of the tepid water.

"We'll wait until dark," I said. "Then we'll see."

By midafternoon, the panic of our near-discovery had worn off, leaving both of us washed with an overwhelming desire to sleep. We sat, legs apart, heads drooping, the heat once again an oppressive weight pressing against us.

The voice was sharp, the snap of a whip. It jerked Sorensen and me up. We struggled to our feet, guns ready. And the voice came again, from the brush. And though I couldn't understand the language, I understood the command.

"Lay your pistol down," I whispered to Sorensen. "Slowly, put it on the deck."

Both of us did so, bending, then straightening, raising our hands by instinct.

There was a rustle in the bush next to our boat, then a man came out, his rifle barrel preceding him. It was one of the Spaniards from the boat. He stepped over the rail, onto the deck, his rifle leveled at me. Then I saw a second one, stepping into the back of the boat. The officer came next, pistol drawn, and stepped aboard behind the first man, who stood just up from the wheelhouse. The officer stepped past him and moved to within arm's length of me.

He was dark from the sun, wore a black mustache, and his eyes were a deep brown. His officer's cap was pulled down low, brimming his forehead, and the pistol was black, a revolver, leveled at my heart.

He spoke, but I didn't know what he was saying. But I knew what he was thinking. His thoughts were written on his face. He very much wanted to kill me.

He spoke again, his voice rising, and I could tell he was asking me a question.

"*No hablo,*" I said, and he hit me.

He used the barrel of the pistol, swinging it backhand, and it struck me just above my right ear. I staggered to my left but didn't go down. I could see flashes of color, bright yellows and oranges.

The officer turned to the soldier behind him and said something, then laughed.

When he turned back to me, Louise's derringer was in

his face, the left barrel not six inches from his forehead. I had reached into my trousers pocket, drawn it out and cocked it in doing so, both hammers, and now I remembered to squeeze only half a pull. The little pistol exploded in my hand, the ball entering the Spanish officer's head just above and between his two eyebrows.

Before he even began his fall, I had the gun on the soldier with the rifle and I fired. The ball hit the man in the throat, passing all the way through and out the back of his neck. He had a startled look on his face. He fired his rifle almost as an afterthought, then dropped it and reached up to his throat with his right hand before crumpling to the deck.

The bullet from his rifle clipped my left shoulder, then went on, I assumed, out into the bay. But it had taken a piece of me with it. I staggered, then dropped to my knees.

The man at the back of the boat was coming up now, moving through the narrow walk between the wheelhouse and the port rail, and as he came around the wheelhouse, Sorensen shot him three times. Sorensen had dropped down, retrieved his pistol, and was waiting for the Spanish soldier, who lurched, hit the wall of the wheelhouse, then bounced back, over the rail and into the water.

I picked up my pistol off the deck.

"There's another one," I said to Sorensen. "Up in the trees. Come on."

I pushed the pistol into my waist and reached up to staunch the blood from my shoulder.

"Get the rifle," I said to Sorensen, as I clambered over the rail into the brush.

Sorensen behind me, I began moving through the tangle of brush and trees, away from the boat. I ducked and dodged, went about fifty steps, then stopped. I raised my hand, and I could hear Sorensen behind me. I turned to look at him, and he had stopped, his pistol in his right hand, the rifle in his left. I put my finger to my lip, indicating to Sorensen to be quiet.

Then I listened.

I could hear the other Spanish soldier. He was running, or trying to, off to the right, no more than a hundred yards from us.

"Give me the rifle," I whispered to Sorensen. He handed it to me. "Take my pistol. Give me yours." We traded pistols. "You've got six shots now." I motioned with the rifle. "He's over there. You circle around that way. I'll go this way. We'll get him between us."

Sorensen, crouching, started off.

"Sorensen?" He stopped, looked at me. "Be careful," I said. "Let's don't shoot each other."

I moved as quickly as I could, as quietly as I could. The jungle was deep in shadow, not a breath of air. I stopped every ten paces, listened, then moved again. At one point, I pulled my shirt from my waist, tore off a piece, folded it, and stuck it inside my shirt, against the wound, hoping it would at least slow the blood. It hurt at the touch, ached too, and I could feel the ache down my left arm.

Then I heard the Spaniard again, moving fast now, raising a ruckus. He was panicked, trying to make their boat.

I moved toward the sound. I couldn't see anything more than twenty feet ahead of me, just a maze of green and shadow. But I knew I was gaining on the soldier. His sound was getting closer and closer.

Then, when I couldn't have been more than fifty yards from him, I heard a shot, then another. Then quiet, then two more shots.

Quietly as I could, I moved toward the sounds of the guns. In a few minutes, I came upon the results.

The Spaniard was dead, lying on his back in a pile of leaves, blood seeping from his chest. Sorensen stood above him, pistol in hand.

"Are there any more?" Sorensen asked.

"I don't think so. Are you hit?"

"No."

"He fired at you?"

"Twice," Sorensen said.

We stood there above the dead Spaniard, in the quiet of the jungle, the only sound our breathing, heavy and quick.

Sorensen looked at me, a small, quirky grin on his face.

"Damn, Sorensen," I said.

———

It was dark before we finished our grisly task of disposing of our afternoon's work. First, we found the Spanish boat, a half mile west of us. In the cabin, Sorensen found iodine and a roll of cloth bandage. He helped me slip off my shirt. The bullet had just nicked my shoulder, leaving a bloody groove, which Sorensen doused with iodine. It stung like hell. Then he wrapped it, using another piece of my shirt as a pad directly on the wound. The bandage was about four feet long, and Sorensen used it all, tying it off above the wound.

Then we moved the Spanish boat. We moored it next to our craft, fished the dead Spaniard out of the water, and placed his body in the cabin. We did the same with the other two bodies, then went up into the jungle to retrieve the fourth. It was a hellish task hauling it back through the brush, dropping it, stumbling, falling. We were white with exhaustion when we finally got it onto the Spanish boat.

Sorensen said he could swim, so just at dark, he took the Spanish boat and its ugly cargo five hundred yards out, and using one of the rifles, he shot out the hull beneath the small engine. We had tied the corpses to the base of the wheel in the cabin so they wouldn't float to the top, and when the boat had filled enough to settle, Sorensen waited until it just began to slip beneath the surface, pushed off, and swam back to our boat. I helped him aboard.

I found a clean shirt in the cabin, one of Humphries's, I figured, and after washing myself off with seawater, I crumpled up my bloody shirt and stuck it behind the coal bin in the wheelhouse.

All that was left of the Spaniards was their blood, which stained the decks of Humphries's boat, already turned black in color.

During the night, I heard Sorensen. He was at the back of our boat, crying.

———

The next morning, we were in a state of gloom. We were far past any sort of excitement now, past even any understanding. Sorensen had entered into that twilight world of soldiers who have taken lives. Any thrill was gone, the drama dwindled to mere memory, mostly bad. I didn't know what Sorensen remembered, but I remembered being afraid. And my shoulder hurt like hell.

We sat, in the still morning, at the prow of the boat, neither of us talking. We stared instead out at the water of the small bay, each of us wrapped in deep thought.

Finally, after a half hour of silence, I said to Sorensen, "They were soldiers, Steven. They wore a uniform. They knew they could die. It's a choice they made."

He looked at me, his face a veil of despair.

"I killed them," he said.

"Yes."

He turned his face away from me and looked out at the water.

———

"He's gone," said Humphries.

"Who's gone?" I asked.

"Maceo. He's in Jamaica. He left a week ago."

Humphries had arrived just at sunset. I spotted him walking toward us on the beach. Now, on board, he didn't seem to have changed much.

Humphries went on. "His boys have quit."

"All the rebels have quit?"

"Maceo's bunch was the last to put up a fight. Somebody got to somebody. Maceo left before anybody could get to him."

"So we aren't the only people after him," I said.

"He's got a huge bounty on his head," Humphries said. "There is no telling how many people are trying to kill him."

"So the war is over?"

"Of course not, old chum. This is just a time-out."

He looked up at Sorensen, who was still sitting on the bow, looking out at the bay. "What's the matter with him?"

"Something he ate," I said. "Or didn't eat. We're tired of these damned sardines."

"Let's go to Key West, then," Humphries said. "Get some decent grub."

It was still light enough to see, and Humphries saw: the dried blood on the deck.

"What's this?"

I told him. It took about five minutes.

"Get this trash off the boat," he said, referring to our camouflage. "We're casting off now."

"You think they'll come?" I asked.

"When that boat doesn't come back, yeah. They'll send a battle cruiser."

And thus our departure from Cuba, made in haste, the mission scrubbed, nothing to show for our effort but four dead men, dead for nothing.

By morning we were well away from Cuba, the day promising to be bright and clear. Our small craft beat a pleasant rhythm to the waves, aided by a wind from the east, a trade wind that was profit. Humphries and I had let Sorensen sleep through the night, dividing the watches between the two of us. Humphries knew what was bothering the little Michigan tadpole. Humphries had probably been there himself.

Now, the sun warm at our backs, Sorensen and I sat again on the prow of the ship, feeling the wind and the occasional spray from the wash of the bow.

"Sorensen?"

He looked at me, looking a lot better now than he had the night before.

"That was something," I said. "The way you handled that pistol."

He smiled.

I asked, "Where did you learn to shoot like that?"

"You taught me," he said.

"I didn't teach you to shoot like that."

He was quiet a bit, then looked again to the front. "No," he said, "it was fear. When you shot those two Spanish bastards, all I could think of was the one at the back. I knew he would come. I knew he would kill me."

"Kind of an either/or thing," I said.

"And the one in the bush—" Sorensen turned to look at me. "He had two shots at me. That was more than fair."

"Yeah," I said. "It was."

"Where'd you get that little gun?" he asked.

"It belongs to Louise," I said.

Sorensen looked at me a few seconds, then said, "Figures."


## X.


HUMPHRIES, naturally, knew of the best doctor in Key West, a fellow named Chavez, who, oddly enough, wasn't Cuban but American, from Philadelphia. Dr. Chavez took one look at my shoulder wound and pronounced it superficial. Nonetheless, he reopened it, slipping off the already forming scab, and doused it with a fine and bad-smelling yellow powder, then re-dressed it. He gave me a vial of the powder, told me to apply it every twenty-four hours, and Humphries gave him a crisp, new hundred-dollar bill.

"That's a lot of money," I said to Humphries when we left Chavez's office.

"An investment, sport," Humphries said. "The doctor is good with gunshot wounds and is very discreet."

We had arrived in Key West the day before and had spent the night in a fine little cottage on the outskirts of town, a white clapboard abode snuggled down against a beautiful white sand beach. It was, Humphries said, home. Elegantly furnished, one room was filled with nothing but guns and boxes of cartridges. There were also several small kegs of black powder. Sorensen noted that, despite its charm, the cottage held the singular distinction of being a place that could, even on a whim, be blown to smithereens. This explosive fact did not, however, prevent his rest, and Sorensen was asleep shortly after sunset and still asleep the next morning when Humphries and I set out for our visit to Dr. Chavez. He was lazing about the front porch when Humphries and I returned, drinking a cup of coffee and smoking a morning cigar.

"You still have your arm," he said, as I pulled up a chair to sit with him. "Good news."

"Gentlemen," Humphries said, "if you will excuse me, I have a bit of business to transact in town. Do make yourselves at home, and help yourselves to the larder. I believe you will find something to your liking there."

And he was off, walking his brisk, Yale-ish step toward the city.

"Coffee?" Sorensen asked me.

"No, thanks," I said.

We sat back, watching the water as it lapped against the beach.

Eventually, Sorensen said, "We've failed miserably, you know."

"Yes."

"Nothing to show for any of this."

"What will you tell your father?"

"The truth," Sorensen said. "Maceo wasn't there." Then he asked, "Would you have done it? Would you have killed him?"

"No."

Sorensen looked out at the water. "Me neither," he said.

Home. That was the issue now, the only issue.

"A packet for Boston," Humphries said, our second day in his humble little abode. "Sails tomorrow on the tide. I've arranged passage for you boys."

Humphries made the announcement over our prone bodies. Sorensen and I had been asleep on the floor mats in what usually served as Humphries's living room. It was, oddly enough, late afternoon. Time, ever since we'd left Providence days and days before, was out of joint.

"But first," Humphries said, "a farewell dinner, at Mamacita's, the best food in the Florida Keys. Gentlemen, we won't be dressing for dinner. Though I do suggest you bathe in the sea."

We did dress, after we'd bathed. Humphries had clothes, which he loaned to Sorensen and me. Quality cloth, tailored in Havana, Humphries claimed. So, with creased trousers and fine white shirts, Sorensen and I rode with Humphries in a hired carriage to the west side of the city, the "deeply Cuban side," as Humphries called it. And there, in what looked like a prestigious private dwelling, was Mamacita's.

"This is somebody's house," Sorensen said, as we lighted down from the carriage.

"To the tourists," Humphries said. "Keeps out the riffraff."

We passed through a gated passage into a cool, shady courtyard, where there was a fountain, an actual fountain shaped as a star, with water cascading down. Beyond the fountain were three tables, where we were met by a large mulatto woman, in her fifties, I guessed.

"*Bon soir, Monsieur Humphries. Comment allez-vous, ma cher?*"

Mamacita, it turned out, was French Creole, from, Humphries explained after we'd been seated, Haiti.

The aperitifs were a pleasant concoction of sugar, lime, and rum, chilled even, and the meal was roast pork, layered and braised, served with a fine mint sauce. There were also fried plantains, rice seasoned with peppers, black beans and onion, pickled okra, baked yams, and a delicious brown bread smothered in butter. A beautiful, dark woman with flashing black eyes kept our cups filled with a fine, chilled rosé.

Dessert was pie, kiwi pie in a heavy custard base.

Nobody talked. All we did was eat.

The ride back to Humphries's house was made in a pleasant cloud of quality tobacco smoke.

At rest on the porch facing the sea, the evening spread out against the sky, a near full moon rising in the east.

"Beats the hell out of sardines and crackers," Sorensen said, working on his second cigar of the evening and sipping some of Humphries's select brandy.

"She's a high priestess, you know," Humphries said. "Mamacita. In the African-Franco Church of the Antilles. Voodoo. She can cure or kill anything."

We sat, the three of us, in wicker chairs, smoking, drinking, savoring the evening.

"*Señor* Humphries," Sorensen said, "you are a character from a novel, a very bad novel."

"Gentlemen," Humphries intoned. He was slightly drunk. "In a world bereft of value, all that truly matters is . . . style."

"Who told you for us to kill Maceo?" I asked.

"Pardon?" Humphries said.

"It wasn't the Army, was it?"

"My dear fellow, what difference does it make?"

"Who gave the order?" I asked. There was just a slight edge in my voice.

"Crofton," Sorensen said, "what are you doing?"

"Was it your idea?" I asked Humphries. "Were you doing it for your Spanish pals?"

Humphries wasn't drunk any longer. Beneath all his

charm and his style and his savoir faire, he was a dangerous man, dangerous as a snake.

I was sitting only a few feet from him, and even in the dim light of the moon and the distant light of the city, I could tell he was thinking, a slight smirk on his face, his eyes focused and tight.

"We didn't kill him," Sorensen said. "He wasn't even there."

"But somebody wanted him dead," I said. Then, to Humphries: "Who?"

Humphries spoke, his voice even and still. "You know your problem, Crofton? You're a moral man." He paused. "That's a shame."

"I will not murder," I said.

He got up, and I tensed. But he turned and went into his house.

"Jesus, Crofton," Sorensen whispered. "We're leaving tomorrow. Let it rest."

Humphries returned with a lighted candle in a holder and a piece of paper. He set the candle on the small wicker table next to my chair and handed the paper to me. It was folded.

I unfolded it and read it by the light of the candle.

Sorensen and Crofton to arrive May 15 stop To attend AM funeral stop No toys for AM friends.
Sherman

I looked up at Humphries, who had reseated himself.

"Sherman ordered it?"

"Uncle Billy himself," Humphries said.

Sorensen got up, came over, took the telegram from my hand. After he read it, he asked, "What does this mean?"

I said, "General Sherman ordered you and me to kill Maceo. And he told Humphries not to let the rebels have the guns."

"Satisfied?" Humphries said.

Still holding the telegram, Sorensen sat back down in his chair.

"Jesus," he said. "Now even Sherman is going to be mad at us."

———

He lay, the little plop, on his back, his tiny arms and legs flailing. Naked, his skin was a creamy white and as smooth as smooth is. His eyes were taking on a blue tint now, and his hair had turned too, a lighter color. And he'd gained weight, three pounds, his mama said.

We lay together on the bed in my father's house, the afternoon sunlight sliding through the window, festooned with tiny silver flashes, motes and such. He made a gurgling noise occasionally, and he tried his best to make eye contact with me, but his focus wasn't mastered yet, and he'd go back to looking every which way, but the arms and legs still flailed about.

I don't think I'd ever seen anything quite so beautiful, except maybe his mother when she, too, was naked and lying beside me.

Home. I was home, with my son.

# Three

## I.

"THERE ARE ONLY twenty-five thousand people in the Army," Sorensen said.

I looked at him over the grave.

"How do you know that?" I asked.

"A fellow in the paymaster's office told me."

It was cold, a brisk wind coming up the Potomac off Chesapeake Bay. Sorensen and I were dressed in heavy blue issue coats, and we wore warm leather gloves, but none of it cut the wind. We were leveling headstones at Arlington Cemetery. It was December.

Sorensen said, "You know what that means, don't you?"

"What?"

"This is what we are going to be doing. This is what our careers are going to amount to. Tending the dead."

"Beats getting shot at," I said.

Since Sorensen and I had returned from our inglorious trip to Cuba, we hadn't maximized opportunities. If anything, we had done just the opposite. We had interviewed with Colonel Small about our mission, raising his hackles with the news of the four dead Spanish soldiers. He had harangued us about being sent to Cuba precisely to end a war, not start one. We then learned that our jobs in the War Department had been taken by a couple of shiny second lieutenants just out of the academy. And through the summer and into the fall, we had been shuffled around the forts surrounding Washington, assigned to no-account jobs such as sorting and packing uniforms, inventorying bridle and harness, and counting empty beds in barracks. We had finally achieved semipermanent positions in Maintenance and Supply, which, for the foreseeable future, meant taking care of graves and grounds at Arlington Cemetery.

But we weren't the only ones suffering ignominy. Sorensen's father had apparently fallen out of favor with the Hayes administration and had lost his committee seat. Sorensen told me he was drinking and sending morose letters back to his wife, Sorensen's mother, in Michigan. Naturally, he blamed his political misfortune on Sorensen and me. As he put it to Steven, "This is what happens of sending boys to do a man's work."

Through it all, though, I was happy. I had Louise, I had Darien, and our little nest on M Street was an island of harmony in a sea of disappointment. And the baby was growing. At seven months, he was sitting up, crawling, and grinning. He was one happy child, nursing regularly and romping with me in the evenings.

"And how come we ain't got some enlisted men for this?" Sorensen asked, above the wind.

"There aren't any," I said, using my bar to shift a headstone to an upright position.

"So two officers do the work."

"A democratic army," I said.

Sorensen was bitter, not used to manual labor, and not used to cold. "They're busting caps all over the west, killing redskins, and what are we doing? Grave diggers."

"Hey," I said, "look at this one. A Reb."

The stone read:

UNKNOWN CONFEDERATE SOLDIER
1865

"Well, that's great," Sorensen said. "First we kill the sons of bitches, and then we have to bury them."

It was getting on toward evening, and the sky was turning darker and darker. Sorensen and I were alone in the vast field, headstones and empty space. We could see the capitol across the river, and behind us Lee's mansion rose like a monolithic reminder of some hard and lost cause. There was nobody about. The wind was gradually shifting around to the north.

"Texas," Sorensen said. I looked at him. "That's where we ought to go. Texas."

"Why?" I asked.

"Cattle," he said. "Get a herd, put them on a boat, and take them to Key West."

"We know so much about cattle and boats."

"Aw, Crofton, you're a moron."

"I'm not moron enough to go to Texas."

Later, at supper, though, Louise gave Sorensen's idea a boost.

"That's not a bad idea," Louise said.

"What?" I said.

"I told him," Sorensen said.

We sat at the supper table. Sorensen and I were eating. Louise was nursing Darien.

"My daddy bought Texas cattle," Louise said. "Well, actually, he stole them. Kind of."

"Louise," I said, "what are you talking about?"

"In the Panhandle, that part of Texas they call the Panhandle. Wild cattle, though everybody claims them. Daddy got some old buffalo hunters together, and we all went down there and rounded up almost a hundred head. Moved them up to Dodge City and sold them."

Sorensen was excited now. "You made money?" he asked Louise.

"Well, not exactly. There was this Texas sheriff waiting for us. He took the money. He would have hanged Daddy if we hadn't lit out. He did hang one of the buffalo hunters."

"But there were cattle," Sorensen said.

"Five dollars a head," Louise said. "That's what the man in Dodge City paid."

"Damn," said Sorensen. "In Key West, we could get twenty."

In truth, I couldn't see Sorensen and me as cattle barons. And I knew enough of Texas to reckon rough people, hard country, and evil weather. Yet Louise seemed delighted by the idea, and Sorensen was sufficiently perturbed to do most anything. My consolation amidst the turmoil of wild ideas was the Army. Sorensen and I were in the Army. We were under obligation, at present, to fix gravestones, to tend ground. Traipsing off to Texas to risk hanging wasn't really an option for us.

"Sorensen?"

"What?"

"Pass the peas."

So the idea simmered. The next day, Sorensen and I were back among the dead.

"Look at this place," I said. We stood, metal bars in hand, on a small rise overlooking the cemetery. Acres of ground, it wasn't a tenth filled. "It will be full someday, full of graves. Can you imagine?"

The weather had passed, the gray skies gone. Even the wind had died, and now a pale sunlight cast an anemic glow upon the brown grass, the gray headstones, the black of the distant trees.

Sorensen said, "I can imagine greenback dollars, a stack of them—no, several stacks of them. And Key West and beefsteak and good cigars."

There were graves, scores of them, the graves of men killed in the War of the Rebellion. And I'd heard there was even a bigger cemetery up in Pennsylvania at Gettysburg. As Sorensen and I walked the avenues between the stones, pushing one and another into upright positions, poking the ground to make it even, lingering among the ghosts of dozens of battlefields, I couldn't help but wonder at the war I had missed.

Toward noon, Sorensen and I broke for lunch.

"I had this sergeant in Kansas," I said to Sorensen. "He'd been with Grant on the push through the Wilderness in sixty-four. Went all the way to Appomattox a year later. He told some tales."

We were sitting, our backs against a rail fence, eating the sandwiches that Louise had fixed for us. At midday, we'd made the morning.

"Everything was the Army then," I said. "Everybody was in the Army. Thousands and thousands of men. You and I would have been brevet colonels, commanding regiments. The sergeant told me that during the first battle of the Wilderness, nobody could see anything. There was shot and shell coming from all directions. The trees were firing. Think of it—fifty, sixty thousand men in the tangle, firing, loading, firing again. Trees and brush caught fire, and during the night, wounded burned alive. McCallum said he could still hear their cries.

"There wouldn't be a safe place. Those Enfields were accurate up to nine hundred yards. At West Point, you know what they told us? That nearly every general, especially the Northern ones, was using Napoleon's tactics. Bunch the men, get them within a hundred yards of the enemy line, and fire for effect. And the other side with weapons accurate up to nine hundred yards."

I was caught up now in a reverie that only a graveyard could induce. There were hundreds of dead soldiers beneath my feet, men not unlike Sorensen and me, nearly all of them young, their lives gone, snuffed out in the great slaughter.

"All of this," I said, gesturing with my half-eaten sandwich, "this empty ground, crammed full of corpses. There will be men like you and me tending graves ad infinitum. And when this ground is full, they'll find more ground. And the whole world, farmland, ranchland, land where there are houses now, will be one huge cemetery."

I looked at Sorensen. "And all the dead will be honored," I said.

I had, for comfort, my wife. In the dark, we lay together, a cold wind blowing outside, but we were tucked under a pile of blankets, each warm to the touch of the other. Little Darien sometimes slept with us if it was cold, his cradle next to the bed not warm enough. We'd slip him in between our naked bodies and he'd sleep there, like a little purring kitten, while his mother and I kissed or just snuggled.

That was when, the night outside, the baby inside, the world a far and distant remove, we talked, she and I.

"Down there in Cuba," Louise said.

"Yes?" I said.

"Did Steven do all right?"

"He did fine."

"He's going to Texas."

"You think so?" I asked.

"Yes."

I drew her to me in the dark, little Darien form-fitting between us.

"I'm not," I said.

"I know," she said.

The last day of 1878, I reenlisted for four more years. Sorensen resigned his commission. We'd gone down to the War Department to do our business, early, a bitterly cold day. Afterward, down at the Murray Hotel, we had hot rum in the bar.

Sorensen said, "You're making a mistake."

"No."

"Texas, son. Wild people, wild cattle, a fortune to be made."

"Steven, go by way of Kansas City. When you get there, ask for a man named Cyrus Rill. If you find him, tell him your plan."

"Rill?"

"Yes," I said. "He's a good man."

"Crofton?"

"Yeah?"

"Down there in Cuba." I watched him across the table. The light was dim in the bar, but I could see that he was struggling with something. "Well, down there in Cuba," he said.

"Yes," I said. "I know."

"So it's Texas now," he said, grinning.

"Be careful, Sorensen. Those Texans are hard people."

"I'll do all right," he said.


II.


SNOW CAME. It was a heavy, wet snow. There was a caretaker cabin to the east of the cemetery. It had a couple of windows, a slanted roof, and a coal stove. I waited out the storm there. It had taken me two hours to walk from home to Arlington, a trip that usually took forty-five minutes. I sat in the cabin, in a straight-backed chair, warm from the stove, and watched the snow out the window. It fell straight down. There was no wind.

At midday, out the window, I saw a man, tall, thickset. He was wearing a heavy coat and cape and had a broad black hat pulled down. He wandered up from the north side of the cemetery, tramping through the snow in heavy black boots. He was no more than a hundred yards from the cabin. He came to a rise, from which he could survey the cemetery, the headstones just beginning to disappear, the Lee mansion beyond but barely visible in the fall of the snow. And there he stood, simply looking. I watched him for a while, then got up from my chair and moved to the door of the cabin.

I stepped outside and called to the man.

"Sir?" But he didn't hear me, though it was as quiet as night, the snow muffling sounds. I called again, "Sir!" Louder this time.

He turned, looked at me. I was wearing only my tunic, no cap.

"Can I help you, sir?"

He only stared at me and didn't move. It was as if he had been caught unaware, and he was assessing the situation now.

"I have a stove here," I shouted. "Come, get warm."

He began moving toward me.

He had an immense dark beard, and with his hat pulled down, all I could see of his face were his eyes, dark eyes, but bright, alert.

"Who are you?" he asked, his voice deep and low.

"Lieutenant Michael Crofton, U.S. Army. I'm in charge of these grounds."

"They're open to the public?"

"Yes, sir."

He stood silently, looking at me, then at the cabin, the door open.

I said, "Come inside, sir. Warm yourself. I have coffee."

Inside, the cabin seemed much smaller. He wasn't a particularly tall man, just big. He had used his hat to brush off the snow from his coat, but there still lingered traces of it, and in the warmth of the cabin, those traces rose as small rivulets of steam, rising from the dark cloth.

I did have coffee, a pot, and four cups. I poured one for the visitor.

"I'm sorry," I said, "but I have neither sugar nor milk."

I handed him the cup.

He stood then, his hat in one gloved hand, his cup in the other. His dark hair, streaked with gray, was plastered against his head. There were spots of moisture in his immense gray-black beard.

"This is easy duty you have here, Lieutenant," he said.

"Yes, sir."

I offered him the one chair, but he shook his head no.

"I came out to see the graves," he said. "I have been told there are Southern soldiers buried here."

"Yes, sir, quite a few."

"Where are you from, son?"

"Rhode Island, sir."

"You were too young for the war."

"Yes."

"And this has been your post?" he asked.

"I was with the Seventh Cavalry, in Kansas."

"With Custer?"

"Yes, sir."

He sipped his coffee. "A bad end there."

He put his hat on the small table, his cup too, and removed his gloves, laying them beside his hat. He offered me his hand.

"I'm James Longstreet," he said.

"Sir," I said, taking his hand.

———

General James Longstreet had been Robert E. Lee's right-hand man after the death of Stonewall Jackson. Lee called him his War Horse. Longstreet had been with Lee at Gettysburg, and in the terrible year and a half afterward, always loyal, always there, for General Lee and for the South.

The general was in town now, of all things, to look for a job. He was living in Georgia and was hoping to become a U.S. Marshal. He had been to the Justice Department, asking around. He was due to leave that night on a train for the South.

"Did you have any luck?" I asked about his job search.

"It remains to be seen," he said.

"I suppose something like that is a political matter."

"Yes."

He was sipping on his second cup of coffee.

"Did you walk here, sir?" I asked.

"I have a horse. He's tethered at the gate. I must see to him."

"The snow is unusual," I said. "We've had a mild winter."

Longstreet gestured slightly toward the window and the cemetery beyond. "This will all be soldiers?" he asked.

"Yes, sir, a military cemetery."

"There's one at Gettysburg," he said.

"I've heard that."

"All the boys are buried together, blue and gray."

There was a wistfulness in his voice, a dreamy quality, making him sound almost hoarse.

I didn't speak. There was nothing I could say. This man, this General of the Confederacy, had ridden out in a snowstorm to see this ground. It was a duty for him. His presence alone spoke more than either he or I could say.

"I must be going," he said, rising.

He shook my hand again before putting on his gloves. Then, with his hat in place, I opened the door for him. He stepped out. I followed. He looked to his left, but all was covered by snow now. He turned back to me.

I saluted.

He touched his hat and walked away.

## III.

CAREERS WERE being made in the West, what careers there were and what careers there were to be made. The Indian wars were the only wars. And for the first time in the history of the republic, an equation had become unbalanced. There were too many soldiers and not enough Indians. Since the previous summer, I had repeatedly asked for a transfer to a post beyond the Mississippi. I had reasoned that my experience with the 7th Cavalry would be of use on the plains, where the last aborigines were fighting the last battle. But I had repeatedly been told that lieutenants were in ample supply on the frontier. Privates were what the Army needed out there.

My current assignment was to the D.C. Supply and Maintenance Depot, a churlish organization headed by a Colonel Dupree, a tottering old gent who had an office in the administration building at Fort Belvoir near Alexandria. Dupree had been a supply officer as far back as the Buchanan administration and had spent the whole of the War Between the States in Washington. His specialty was shoes. He had shod legions of Union infantry only to discover at war's end that that he was overinventoried in shoes but faced with a dwindling number of feet to put them on.

He had, in time, forsaken his duty to feet and adopted a new duty, the preservation of Colonel Alexander Dupree's career. He became then one of the Army's most notable deviants, a career officer who had absolutely no value whatsoever.

"The Indians will remain unrepentant savages," Colonel Dupree announced, "until they start wearing shoes."

I sat, a cold January afternoon, in Colonel Dupree's office, bearing my latest petition for transfer.

"Do you know," Colonel Dupree said from behind his desk, "what separated the Romans from the hordes of barbarians that they slaughtered and conquered?" He paused for dramatic effect. "Sandals."

I guessed Dupree to be in his sixties, though he looked much older. A red-veined face, balding head, and eyebrows that grew at cockamamy angles. He had, in truth, the visage of a demented frog.

"My service, sir," I said, "with the Seventh Cavalry specifically, recommends me for a transfer to a Western command."

"Horses," Dupree said. "Even horses need shoes. The mark of civilization, Lieutenant."

"My transfer?"

"Will be forwarded," he said.

"As all the others."

"Exactly."

"Colonel Dupree?"

"Yes."

"Do you know anyone in the West? An officer with whom you have a friendly relationship?"

I was hoping for a wild card in the dull and profitless game I was playing.

He thought, thought, then thought some more.

"No," he said, "I don't believe I do." Then he added, as a poignant afterthought, I'm sure, "Napoleon had it all wrong. An army does not move on its stomach. An army moves on its feet."

"You're absolutely right, Colonel," I said.

"Glad you agree, Lieutenant. Glad you agree."

And he took my request for transfer and put it in a drawer.

Louise was sympathetic.

"Do you want Darien and me to come to the cemetery with you?" she asked over supper.

"Come where the fighting is the thickest, huh?" I said.

"There is no one else there, is there?"

"Just dead folk."

"We can push Darien in the pram. I can make sandwiches."

The pram, I thought. Sandwiches. A family outing.

Louise said, "You won't be so lonesome that way."

"Wouldn't want a soldier to be lonesome," I said.

Oh glory. Oh honor. Oh duty. Oh country.

"That would be nice," I said. "When it gets a little warmer. There are some fine spots for picnicking. When it gets a little warmer."

She reached across the table and touched my hand.

It was a cold, gray day, old snow not yet begun to melt. I sat in my useless little cabin drinking my third cup of coffee. Then I heard it, the report of a rifle. It couldn't have been very far away. I stood up, listening and peering out the two windows, one on each opposite east/west wall. Then I heard another shot.

I slipped on my coat, gloves, and hat. There was an ordinance specifically forbidding the discharge of firearms in the cemetery.

As I stepped out into the cold, I heard a third shot, and though I was certain it wasn't directed at me, I still flinched, an old soldier's habit.

The gun was being fired off to my right, and I tramped through the snow in that direction. Moving up a rise of ground, I heard yet another rifle shot, and once atop the rise, I could see. There were five men down in a small draw. They all wore the uniform, and one, a slim, small fellow, had a rifle. He was firing at a wooden box fifty yards from him, up against a snowbank.

I moved down toward the men. The shooter raised his rifle and fired again, and as I was within shouting distance, I did exactly that.

"Hey!"

All of the men turned to look at me.

Moving toward them at a determined pace, I shouted

again, "What are you doing? You can't fire that weapon here."

One of the men, a short, squat fellow, moved away from his companions and walked toward me. As he got closer, I could see he was wearing Army-issued clothing.

"Hello there," he said, not twenty yards from me.

And with that, the rifle went off again with a piercing roar.

"Stop that shooting!" I yelled. I brushed past the squat fellow, making a beeline for the man with the rifle.

The rifleman must have heard the tone of my voice, because he lowered the rifle and turned to look at me.

I was next to him in twenty steps, and I grabbed the rifle. Jerking it from his grasp, I said, "I told you not to shoot. This is a cemetery, not a firing range."

"Who, sir," the man said, "are you?"

I unbreeched the rifle. The empty cartridge casing popped out.

"I'm the one," I said, staring fiercely at the fellow, "who told you to stop shooting. Who are you?"

"Sherman," he said. "William Sherman, and I would like my rifle back."

"General Sherman?"

"My rifle?" he said, holding his hand toward me.

"General, sir," I said. "I'm sorry. But you can't discharge firearms in the cemetery." And I still held the rifle.

He had a scruffy beard, and he wasn't wearing a hat. His hair was a sandy orange color, but yellow and gray in places. He was thin, but made to look heavier by the winter coat he wore.

He smiled at me. "Who are you, sir?" he asked.

"I'm Lieutenant Crofton. I'm in charge here."

"So I see," he said.

The other men had moved up, and I found myself at the center of a small circle.

Sherman told the other men, "The lieutenant says we aren't allowed to discharge firearms in the cemetery." With a mischievous look in his eye, he added, "I do believe he means it."

Sherman reached inside his coat and pulled out a cigar. One of the other men produced a matchbox, scratched one, and held it for the general. Drawing his head back and emitting a stream of smoke, the general looked at me.

"Do you know what kind of rifle that is?" he asked. "It is a Martini-Henry carbine, the M-H Mark One. It fires a Short Chamber Boxer-Henry forty-five caliber black-powder cartridge. It is the weapon of choice of the British Army. And a fine gun it is." He gestured toward the snow back where the target box was. "If you will examine that wooden box, you will see that it causes considerable damage."

I handed it back to him.

"Thank you, Lieutenant," he said.

———

The commander of the U.S. Army and I had coffee. He sat, I stood, in the little cabin. His entourage waited outside.

Sherman said, "You and . . . what's his name? Went down to Cuba, right?"

"Sorensen, sir. Yes, we did."

"To kill that fellow Maceo."

"On your order, sir."

"Yes," the general said. "Fine soldier, that Maceo fellow. A burrhead general. Missed him, though." He sipped his coffee, pulled at his half-smoked cigar. "But I hear you killed some Spaniards."

"Yes, sir," I said, "by accident."

"Ha! Indeed. Four of them. Well, so be it. You know, we are going to fight those bastards sooner or later. Four less to fight."

"May I ask, General, why you are here?"

"You suspect this is not a social call?"

"I don't think the general came out for target practice."

"Damn fine rifle. Couldn't resist shooting it. But, no, Lieutenant, you're right. I came out to see you."

I said nothing.

General Sherman looked out the east window. "Damn fine idea, this cemetery. Nothing but heroes. Might be buried here myself." Then he looked up at me. "Lieutenant, I want you to go to Africa."

"Africa, sir?"

"The Brits have got themselves into a little war there. With the Nigras. Shouldn't last too long. The Nigras have spears. The Brits have that Martini-Henry."

"Africa, sir?"

"You'll be our liaison there with the Brits. Get the feel for it, the war. Get alongside those boys in the red coats. See how they handle themselves. See how they handle that rifle."

"I'm going as an observer?"

Sherman looked up at me, a look of determination and connivance.

"I want to know about the British," he said, "what they've got, how they use it. Armament especially. I hear they've got an automatic gun, a Gatling. You find out for me. You can't tell, the world being how it is. We might be fighting those limey bastards again. Always good to know your enemies, and your friends. Don't you think?"

He stood up.

"Trip of a lifetime, Sorensen."

"I'm Crofton, sir."

"Yes."

With that, he was out the door.

I stood, my arm frozen in a half-salute.

## IV.

LOUISE WAS pregnant. More than two months along, she said. And there it was again, that dilemma. Why was it that a child always seemed coincidental with my missions to hot lands? After Sherman's executive officer, a Colonel Samuelson, briefed me on my assignment, I had three days to make New York and the sailing of the *Portsmouth Flyer*, an old-fashioned clipper ship bound for London.

Louise took my departure stoically. She took it much better than I did.

"Are you sure you're pregnant?" I had asked.

She hadn't even answered, just looked at me with that men-are-so-stupid look. My mother had that look. I wonder if all women are evolutionarily equipped with it.

There then followed a kind of emotional turmoil, completely unilateral. I was the one felled by anxiety. Louise simply sat, a bewildered Darien on her lap, as I voiced plans, none of which seemed adequate to the situation. I didn't know when I would be back. That was the nexus of the problem. Louise would continue to draw my pay. Samuelson had assured me of that. But what of the baby coming? What of the morning sickness and the strange cravings and hapless sleep schedule?

And what of Darien?

"I've lived with men who would kill you for fifty cents," Louise said, finally. "I think I can live with this."

So she put to flight my ranting.

And there would be the church, the 17th Street Baptist Church, which we attended religiously. It was a mix of blacks and whites, the minister a kindly old white man named Garrison who'd been with John Brown at Harpers Ferry but hadn't been killed or convicted. And there were women in the church, black and white, who thought of Louise as a sister in Christ.

I wrote a hasty letter to my parents, announcing both the coming child and my assignment in the East. And I bought Louise a new pistol, a beautiful little .32 caliber Colt that she greatly admired. It was for ruffians.

I packed my kit. I kissed my son. I hugged and kissed my wife. I caught the train. And I went to New York.

New York Harbor was a forest of spires and funnels. In the cold, clear light of this January morning, there seemed to be a thousand vessels at the docks. I was in uniform, heavy coat, gloves, and visored cap, and carried a large canvas bag as my kit. Though there were a multitude of ships tied up to the docks, there were none out on the bay. How exactly I was to find the *Portsmouth Flyer* was beyond me. All I knew was that it was a clipper ship, not a steamer, but I didn't know a clipper ship from a rowboat. So I did all that I could do—I walked and asked questions.

"Do you know the *Portsmouth Flyer*?" I asked, of this man and that, for over an hour, almost to noon, before finally I met a swarthy black man who pointed. There my vessel was, three ships up.

A beauty—even I, a landlocked footman, thought so. Sleek, low, narrow-hulled, three towering masts. The color of the ship, a burnt brown with white trim, gleamed in the winter sunshine, and a dozen men moved, up two gang-planks, hauling barrels aboard.

A tall fellow in a heavy black coat stood at the back plank, a board in one hand, a pencil in the other. He wore what looked like an officer's hat, and his blond hair flared out beneath it. He was talking to a heavyset, older man, wrapped in a huge fur coat with a Russian hat pulled down over his ears.

I moved close enough to hear their conversation.

"Your rate is too high," the heavy, older man said.

"For winter, sir. That's the rate for winter." The younger fellow wore a smile.

"And you can get her there in a week?"

"God willing."

"I'm paying you," the older fellow said. "Not God."

"And you have insurance, yes? So what's your worry, old man?"

The old man made a humphing sound and walked away.

I moved up to the tall fellow.

"Excuse me," I said. "Is this the *Portsmouth Flyer*?"

"It is," he said, turning to me. "And you, sir? Ah, the soldier boy. Well, hello."

"My name is Crofton," I said.

"Loren Gallagher," he said, putting the pencil in his other hand and offering me his right. "I'm the master of the *Flyer*."

We shook hands.

"You're bound for England," Captain Gallagher said. "You have luck, my friend. Few ships going there."

"And you are."

"Absolutely. It's a money trip. High risk, high gain."

"How's that?"

"The North Atlantic, Mr. Crofton. In January, she's an unforgiving wench. She'll take you to the bottom if you give her but a fraction of a chance."

"You're doing it for the money?"

"Aye, there's a fortune here, for the shipper and the ship. The English are paying a premium. It's a war that's give them cause."

"What are you taking them?"

"Gunpowder. A ton of it." He turned to the ship, saying over his shoulder, "Come aboard, sir. We'll stow your gear."

As I walked shakily up the plank, I was thinking to myself, A ton of gunpowder.

Captain Gallagher insisted I eat supper with him that evening. We ate at a tavern near the docks. It was called the Golden Goose. We had pints of ale with the meal, good New England flounder and fried potatoes.

Gallagher was a talker, a hail-fellow-well-met, brimming with enthusiasm, especially for his ship.

"She's the last of the clippers," he said, his tankard of ale poised in midair. "Ah, they were a grand class of vessel. But it's all steam now. The *Cutty Sark,* the *Yankee Clipper,* they're all gone. My *Flyer* is one of the last. Why, I tell you, man, those ships could fly, nineteen knots with a good wind, New York to New Delhi in a hundred days. The

*Flyer* carries forty-eight sails, and damned if we'll fold a one till we get to Plymouth."

He raised his hand to the waiter, put up two fingers, and a few minutes later we were resupplied with ale.

"Steam," Gallagher said. "What is that? A teakettle running a blue-water ship? Why, I tell you, man, out there, a thousand miles from land, it's the wind that rules, God's natural energy. And when one of the clippers catches the wind, why, there's nothing like it. You really do feel as if you are flying. We'll get some of it, this crossing. You'll see."

He raised his cup, took a hefty drink, then, with foam on his upper lip, he smiled at me, a great, beatific, blinding smile of a man who loves what he does.

———

In all my times, a dozen run-ins with wild Indians, even facing Spanish pistols and rifles, I had never been so scared or, for that matter, so sick as I was on the *Portsmouth Flyer* in the North Atlantic in the middle of winter. It was hell—not hot, but cold, not still, but moving, not frightening, but absolutely, profoundly, cataclysmically terrifying.

The ship ran as a bug upon the water, and the water was unforgiving. So was the wind. Mountains of gray-green water stood before us, behind us, beneath us. It crashed upon us. It licked into every crevice of the ship, a living, omnipotent thing, gnashing and roiling, and freezing upon the rigging and ropes.

And when I thought the end was near, a thought I had a thousand times a day, two thousand times a night, I would heave, again, a churlish white liquid devoid of substance, as I ate very little and drank water only when forced to by thirst. But my stomach did not care. It was intent on emptying itself, even when there was nothing to empty.

I was wet, for seven days, and cold, that trembling, bone-deep cold that sets teeth chattering and muscles contracting in useless spasms of protest and despair, fingers and toes without feeling, my face stuck by a thousand needles.

"She's a fussy one, ain't she!" Loren Gallagher yelled above the wind and roar.

The "she" he referred to was the sea that whipped about us in mammoth, maddening swirls.

Gallagher and I stood, precariously, on the aft deck, clinging to a rail as the ship fought its way forward into great walls of water.

Gallagher had said there were forty-eight individual sails on the *Flyer,* and they were all up, all the time, the slim, narrow-hulled little craft a bullet over the water.

We were three days out of New York, somewhere in the mid-Atlantic, and I was convinced that I was as near death as I would ever be.

"This is . . ." I muttered.

"What!" Gallagher yelled.

"This is . . ."

"Speak up, man!"

"Horrible!" I yelled.

He grinned, a flashing, white-toothed crescent in the unforgiving, gray light.

"Aye!" he yelled. "It's that!"

And he flung his head into the wind.

And the ship moved. God almighty, up and over the waves, sliding down the far side of each as a sled down a snowy hill, sails at full billow, the bow crashing with great plumes of foam, the wake visible even in the rough sea. The boat was built for speed, the last of its kind, engineless, its strength, power, and purpose only the wind.

We didn't splinter, we didn't founder, we didn't break apart, and I didn't know, and still don't, why we didn't. By all the laws of physics, the sea should have broken us into ten thousand shards of wood and cloth and broken bones.

And on the seventh day, a day as still and bright as California, though cold and crisp, England was there, before us, a rising black land along the horizon. Half a day later, we were at anchor in Plymouth Harbor.

"There ye go," Gallagher said to me, as I stood ready to depart the ship. "Terra firma, mate."

"Captain?"

"Aye?"

"You love this, don't you?" I said.

"Aye," he said, his face exploding with bright and shining and pure delight.

## V.

I HAD trouble walking. My legs were rubbery. The land didn't move, but I was walking as if it would. Each step was a brace against sudden, unexpected movement, and my knees trembled and my arms were taut. I carried my kit, up on my left shoulder, using my right hand to balance myself, but still, it took a good half hour to wander from the dock up into the town proper. And I was weak from hunger.

I found a pub, went in, stood to see in the shadow.

"My God, man, ye look as if ye've seen a ghost."

"Yes" was all I could say.

"Come here. Lean against the bar, mate, afore ye fall."

I shuffled over, set my kit on the floor, and leaned. Then I took a deep breath.

"A whiskey," the voice said. Though now I could make out its owner. He was the barkeep. He poured a glass of whiskey, set it before me. "Drink it slow, man."

It was warm, and it had a smooth and smoky taste. It was not a whiskey I'd drunk before. But it burned the life back into me on its way down.

"There," said the bartender. "Are ye all right?"

"I am."

I looked around. The pub was empty.

"You've been at sea?" the barkeep asked.

"I've come over from America."

"In the weather?"

"Aye."

He wiped the bar where my glass had set. "Nobody makes the crossing this time of year."

I sipped another sip, felt the heat, swallowed. "I know why," I said.

With that, he smiled. "A Yank. By God. My name's Bristol, Jeremiah Bristol," and he extended a big hand across the bar.

"Crofton," I said. "Michael," taking his hand.

"And you're a soldier?"

"United States Army."

"Well, are you, now? Come to fight the Zulus?"

"Come to watch," I said.

He shook his head. "And you crossed in January. What was your ship?"

"The *Portsmouth Flyer*."

"A steamer?"

"A clipper."

"Oh, my God. A clipper ship? I'll wager she tossed about a bit."

"A bit," I said, sipping again at the whiskey.

The pub, the whiskey, and the fine ham sandwich Bristol made for me brought me back to life. I had another whiskey, then a fine glass of buttermilk that was the best I'd ever drunk.

It was late morning and no one came into the pub. Bristol wanted to know everything about America, and when he learned I'd been with Custer at the Little Bighorn, he lit up like midnight parade. He knew all about Custer. He said it had been a big story in all the London papers. And when I told him that Custer's own men had killed him, he couldn't believe it. Then, when I told him that Custer's whole command had been killed, he did believe it.

"Led them to the merciless savages," Bristol said. "Why, no wonder. It never said that in the papers."

And I was bound for Zululand? Down at the bottom of the world. How was I to get there? Bristol wondered. And when I said I would go with British troops, Bristol said there were departures every day. But first, I told him, I had to get to London. He gave me directions to the train station. He said there was a train at 11:40. I could catch it if I rushed.

I reached into my pocket, took out some coins. "How am I to pay you? I only have American money."

"Not to worry, mate," Bristol said. "Kill me one of those Zulu fellows."

"You're sure?"

"God, Queen, and country, me lad. God, Queen, and country."

———

London was dark, heavy, and menacing in late afternoon, with men and horses cluttering the streets. Carriages, wagons, hacks, the shouts of drivers, the clatter of hooves, and all about, that darkness, caused, I concluded, by the smoke that lingered, wispy and gray, everywhere, the smoke of thousands of chimneys in the January cold.

I had been given an address, on Brayeen Street, near the docks. I found a taxi hack, its driver wearing a stovepipe hat, and told him the address. He looked at me oddly.

"Whut?" he said.

I told him the address again.

"English, guv'ner. Speak English."

Slowly, I announced the address, pausing between each syllable.

"Oy dunno whut your sayin', bloke. Give me it."

I showed him the address.

"Brayeen, aye. Git in."

And off we went, through the teeming streets, the darkness settling, gas lamps beginning to light, and the cold, a damp, chilling cold not unlike that of the North Atlantic.

The whiskey I'd had in Plymouth was gone now, as was the ham and buttermilk, and I felt slightly nauseous and very, very tired. So tired, in fact, that I dozed as I sat in the jolting carriage. I woke with a start when the driver shouted at me.

"Ho, guv'ner! We ayre heere."

I'd changed some American money for some English money at the train station in Plymouth, but I had no idea what any of it meant. Out of the cab, I offered a handful to the driver.

"A bloody frog, ayre ye? Oor a German. Oy'll take a fair amoont." He plucked a bill from my hand. "Und gratuitee, guv'ner." And he plucked another bill.

And with that, he drove off.

I was stopped at a building, immense and white, but gray now in the failing light. Above the door was a sign, which read: "King's Guard." I knocked. No answer. I knocked again. Still no answer. So I tried the door, it opened, and I went in.

There was a hallway, so dark I could barely see, but a light at the far end, toward which I walked. My kit felt like it weighed a ton, and my legs still had that disjointed rubbery feel. At the end of the hall there was what looked like an office, with a small lamp on a desk and behind the desk a man in a dark blue uniform coat, a tangle of black hair, a wonderful sleek mustache, sound asleep.

"Excuse me," I said.

The man slept on.

"Excuse me," I said a little louder.

He woke. Blinked. Looked at me.

"I say, now," he said. "You're coming here to my office and waking me from my nap. What could you possibly want?"

"A bed," I said. "I believe I'm ill."

"This is not a bloody hospital."

"Are you in the Army?" I asked.

"I am," he said.

"What is your rank?"

"I am a sergeant in the King's Guard."

"I am a lieutenant in the United States Army, so why don't you stand up, Sergeant, put yourself in order, and show me a place to bunk."

With that, he smiled, his mustache lengthening itself. "A bloody Yank," he said, rising. "And an officer at that." Fully standing, he said, "And what, sir, may I ask, are you doing here?"

"I've come to help you whip the Zulus."

"Glory be," he said.

*Jan. 21, 1879*
*My Dearest Louise,*

*I've been in London for two days now. It's a dirty, miserable city. And cold, damp and cold. I got here on a sailing ship called the Portsmouth Flyer. Lord, what a trip that was. I thought we'd sink every minute.*

*I'm due to sail on a ship called the Huddleston in two days. It's carrying the 44th King's Guard to the Cape of Good Hope in the south of Africa. I'm told the trip will take ten days. It's a steam ship.*

*I miss you so much. And worry about you. Are you sick mornings? Are you getting rest, food enough? Are the church women looking in on you? Have you heard from Mother?*

*And how is Darien? The little scamp. He was almost walking. Has he taken any steps yet? Why must I miss that? I miss the smell of him, the smooth feel of him, the squinchy way he squeezes his eyes when he smiles or laughs.*

*And I miss you, my darling. Sleeping with you, feeling you there during the night. Oh and the kisses. And all the sweet other.*

*You can write me at the address on this envelope, but I don't know when I will get your mail. By the first week in February I should be in Zululand, wherever that is. I guess this army is no different than any army. Mail is delivered, just God knows when.*

*Take care my sweet. Hug the little jug for me. And you see the doctor, often. I will pray for you. Please pray for me. I will be home. I will be with you and with our precious little family.*

*It's a girl, Louise. I can feel it.*

*Forever yours,*
*Michael*

## VI.

WHEN HMS *Huddleston* crossed the equator, three hundred soldiers of the 44th King's Guard took turns pissing over the rail into the Atlantic. I did my share and let loose a squirt. It was tradition, I was told. The three hundred soldiers and I were sharing cramped quarters in the bowels of the ship, a three-funnel steamer that was an all-purpose naval vessel, doing duty as a troop transport. We carried weapons, too, nine-pound field guns, crates of shot, and gunpowder. All the soldiers had the Martini-Henry rifle and fifty rounds. I had one, too. It had been issued to me by Sergeant Briarmoore, the chap who had welcomed me so auspiciously into the King's Guard my first night in London. He was more or less assigned to me now, though he had a platoon of twenty-six men who occupied him more thoroughly.

We'd left the cold. The weather grew hotter and balmier the farther south we got, and now, at the equator, it was stifling. There could be no sleeping in the hold. Men would have gotten sick from the heat. So the officers had allowed the men topside. The three hundred of us were spread about the aft of the ship like laundry on a lawn. Some had rigged shade with canvas tarps, where we all tried to huddle during the day. At night, it was sleep where you could, and the nights were quite pleasant, the southern sky all aglow with stars, the temperature bearable. The old *Huddleston* made a steady six knots, and the sea was mercifully calm.

The fifth night out, Briarmoore and I sat against a bulkhead on the starboard side of the ship. It was dark and the temperature had dropped. Briarmoore smoked a pipe that gave off a pleasant scent. He had helped me get assimilated into the regiment, introducing me to the officers and other noncommissioned officers. I'd even sat in on a lecture or two about the Guard's mission. The Guard was to reinforce the 24th Regiment, which had been in the Natal area for a year and was now involved in a push into Zululand.

Briarmoore was telling me about his experiences in India.

"Beautiful country," he said, "but poor. Beggars in Calcutta cripple their children so they can earn more begging. Aw, the rot. And those Indian blokes, they hate us whites. Four years I was there, and never saw a friendly brown face."

"It's their country," I said.

"God help 'em if it was. They'd make a muck of it. Those wogs hate each other as much as they hate us. The bloody Moslems hate the bloody Hindus. The bloody Hindus hate the bloody Moslems. And the bloody Sikhs hate everybody."

"So there was nothing good about your time there?" I asked.

"The gin," Briarmoore said.

"So why are you there? Why are the English there?"

"The flag, mate. Another place to put up the flag. March around, sing 'God Save the Queen.' Rob the beggars blind."

"An empire," I said.

"Just like the bloody Romans. Only ours is bigger."

"They say the sun never sets on the Union Jack," I said.

"Aye. And it's blokes like us that got it."

Our sixth day out, we encountered a British merchant

ship northbound. As that steamer grew near, I could make out its name on the bow, *Esmerelda*. It was two stacks, a civilian crew. The *Esmerelda* hailed us, and after a bit of maneuvering, the ships drew alongside each other. Using what looked like a crossbow, a crewman from the other ship shot a bolt over to us. It landed up on the foredeck, where a *Huddleston* man picked it up and took it up to the captain on the bridge.

In about ten minutes, that same crewman waved to the *Esmerelda*, and the little two-funneled freighter pulled away.

The word quickly spread. It came down to Briarmoore and me from a seaman, a little tar not much older than sixteen or so.

"Tragedy," the little fellow said, all dramatically. "A thousand dead. Zulus massacred 'em."

"What are you talking about?" Briarmoore asked.

"Isandlwana," the little seaman said.

There was an officer's call shortly after, and I met with the colonel of the regiment and a handful of other officers in the ship's stateroom. The colonel was named Napejack, and he was a serious man. A professional soldier in his fifties, he was tall and slender and his hair was all white. He wore a stiff khaki tunic and a brown belt down and across his chest. His insignia was silver on his collars.

"Gentlemen," he said when we were all gathered, "the Twenty-fourth Regiment has been decimated at a place called Isandlwana. There are thirteen hundred men lost. It

happened on January twenty-third. The First and Second Battalions went up against an estimated twenty-three thousand Zulus. There was another fight at a place called Rorke's Drift. Our lads held them off there, but at a frightful cost."

He looked at us all, his gaze steady.

"You are to pass this information on to your troops. Don't worry about alarming them. I want them alarmed."

The leftenant in charge of Briarmoore's company was a young fellow, twenty-four or so, named Yancey. He walked with me down the corridor outside the stateroom.

"God," he said. "Two battalions."

"Did you know any of them?" I asked.

"Some. I was at Sandhurst with a few of them. My God, how could something like that happen?"

"Somebody made a mistake," I said, thinking of Custer.

"All those men. And they had rifles. The blacks only had spears."

"Twenty-three thousand spears," I said.

The news cast a pall upon the three hundred Guardsmen aboard ship. Our trip had been a lark before, a Sunday walk to a hot clime. Nobody on board that ship expected something like this. The general feeling, and I had felt it myself, was that the technology of the British would make short work of suppressing a tribe of backwoods savages. The Martini rifle alone, with its lethal .45 caliber slug, seemed quite enough against an enemy who had no firearms at all.

But it was hard to argue against thirteen hundred dead.

"It's all in the numbers," Briarmoore said to me, as we sat beneath the canvas, the equatorial sun casting jagged bright lines upon the water. "If the wogs can mass numbers like that, all the cannon in the world won't help you."

"That's a lot of wogs," I said.

"Those Zulus are killers, too," Briarmoore said. "Tough bastards. Mean as snakes."

"Fighting on their ground."

Briarmoore was silent a bit, then he said, more to himself than to me, "God bless those fellows of the Twenty-fourth."

## VII.

THE COUNTRY on the Natal-Zulu border reminded me of Nebraska: rolling hills and outcroppings, sometimes rising a hundred feet or so, trees only in the wallows. There wasn't a lot of rain, I could tell that, and in February it was hot, summer down under. The King's Guards drew an encampment out on a bald plain, at the edge of an enormous British camp. Briarmoore told me there were regiments coming in from all over. Isandlwana had been an alarm set off all the way from London to Calcutta to Sydney, and British troops were rushed to Natal from around the Empire.

Lt. General Lord Chelmsford was in command. The massacre at Isandlwana was all his, and from the general

look of things, Briarmoore and I figured His Lordship was laying low. He would not underestimate the Zulus again, and when he went at them the next time, he would go in force.

I shared a small tent with Leftenant Yancey. He was a young upstart of a fellow, all creases and buttons, sandy, almost red hair and blue eyes. He looked English, pale like the light there, and stiff, like the people. He hailed from some place called Devonshire, and he'd graduated from Sandhurst, the British West Point. The Army was his ladder, and he had climbed it as far as he could at his age. He loved the Army, I could tell that. Some men do and some men don't, and those who do, like Yancey, see hardship only as opportunity.

"There's a slew of those boys from Rorke's Drift up for the V.C.," he announced to me one dreary afternoon as we sat outside in the shade of our tent.

"The V.C.?" I said.

"The Victoria Cross. It's the boss. Your career is oiled all the way, you get one of those."

"You planning on getting one?"

"I plan on doing my duty."

"You ever been in anything like this, Yancey?"

"A war? No. But I'm trained. I'm ready. You?"

"Just against Indians. They're like the Zulus, maybe not as organized."

"How'd you do?" he asked.

"I didn't get killed."

He was fidgeting with a tent peg, trailing it back and forth in the dust. "Were you ever scared?"

"Terrified," I said.

"Yeah," he said. "I guess one would be."

"Yancey?" He looked at me. "You listen to Briarmoore if things get hot. He's a good man, knows things."

He thought a few seconds, then said, "All right."

The lads drilled. It was the damnedest thing I ever saw. Out there in the heat, marching like on parade, two hours in the morning, two hours in the afternoon. I sat in the shade of a lone tree and watched. I couldn't get the sense of it at first, and then I began to see it. All that marching, their blue tunics buttoned up tight, that white pith helmet on their heads, sweat running in rivulets off their burning faces, the nine-pound Martinis parked on their shoulders, they were getting used to it: the heat, the discipline, the obedience.

Briarmoore was a tyrant. He lashed his platoon with an invective so bitter, so cruel, that he had some of his boys crying, tears running with the sweat off their peach faces. And he didn't let up on them, but would have them quarter arms and do double time until, just at the edge of exhaustion, he'd stop them, put them on the ground, then lecture them as they lay sprawling on the dirt and brown grass, telling them in a voice harsh as the sunlight what shopkeepers they were, clerks with pencils behind their ears, mooning little calves looking for Mother's tit.

Then he'd march them some more, close-order drill, left, right, close it up, close it up.

After one exhausting exercise, he joined me under my tree as his platoon staggered to their tents.

"Pipsqueaks," he said, sitting down, taking off his helmet. "Little boys playing soldier. The Zulus will cook them for breakfast."

I didn't say anything.

"What do you Yanks do?" he asked. "To make men of boys?"

"We do this," I said. "Maybe not as . . . strenuously."

"And you get soldiers?"

I looked at him and grinned. "We beat you chaps, twice."

He smiled, but just a little one.

We stared out at the dusky plain, the light white with the heat.

———

"Crofton! Come on."

Asleep, then awake, I rose up from my cot.

Yancey was standing above me, buckling on a belt and holster. "We're going out. Get dressed."

"Out?"

It was just light outside the tent, the sun not up, a gray haze out on the plain. And it was cold. I couldn't believe it was cold. I sat up.

Yancey said, "We're going out with a couple of Xhosas, scouting."

"X whats?"

"Good blacks."

A captain, a tall fellow with coal-black hair and chin whiskers just as black, had us in his tent, bigger than others, a folding table in the middle, a map on the table. An orderly gave me a spot of tea as the captain told Yancey what he wanted.

There was a sandy river, empty now in the dry season, four miles to the east. There'd been talk of movement there the previous evening. Yancey was to proceed with the Xhosas, see what was there. He was instructed not to engage, just scout and report.

Just before Yancey and I left the tent, the captain took me aside and said to me, "You're doing this on your own."

The Xhosas were a couple of tall, angular fellows, blacker than any of the blacks I'd ever seen. They wore what looked like blankets, wrapped around them and up over one shoulder. They carried old Brown Bess flintlocks, powder and shot in bags slung across their chests. And they were afoot. Yancey and I were on ponies, little things, but quick, frisky in the cold air.

When we set off, the Xhosas broke into a lope, the tops of their heads hardly moving, their long legs striding along. Yancey and I rode at a canter, just keeping up with the blacks.

Yancey had a service revolver, on a lanyard, and I had my Colt. I also had a Martini strapped on my back. Yancey had told me the previous evening that officers didn't carry rifles. I thought that not so smart.

The sun was just breaking the horizon as we left the British encampment behind. It was a monstrous sun, more red than orange, and it slipped up over the flat, arid plain, a great ball of glow.

We rode easy, a half hour, an hour, the Xhosas never breaking stride, and we stopped atop a ridge. Down below us was the riverbed, a mile away, no one there, nor to the north or south either. One thing, I thought, in this country, it would be hard to sneak up on anyone on high ground.

The Xhosas squatted, their bony knees up even with their heads.

"Nothing," Yancey said.

"Let's dismount," I said, "let the horses rest."

Standing, reins in hand, I could feel the first heat of the day on a breeze out of the south.

"There's no one here," Yancey said, a trace of disappointment in his voice.

Yancey spoke to the blacks. "You, boys, you see anything? Zulu?"

They looked at him with big sorrowful eyes and said nothing.

"Damn."

"It's good, Yancey," I said, "that no one's here."

"We're going to go farther," he said, putting his foot in the stirrup and pulling himself up on the pony.

"We weren't told to go farther," I said.

"A few more miles," he said, "over that far ridge, the other side of the river. Then we'll go back."

I reluctantly mounted.

"There," Yancey said to the black, pointing to the east. "We go there."

They looked at each other, then back at Yancey. But they didn't get up.

"Let's go, boys," Yancey said to them.

They still didn't get up. They just squatted there, looking up at Yancey.

"I don't think they want to go, Yancey," I said.

"Well, of course they don't want to go," he said to me. "But they're working for us." He looked down at the Xhosas. "Now, look, fellows, we're going to ride down there to that riverbed, then up to that far ridge. Take a look, then head back. All right?"

They weren't going to do it. I knew that. And so did they. Only Yancey didn't know it.

"Let's go back, Yancey," I said. "We've accomplished our mission. Let's go back, get there in time for lunch."

"Huzzah!" he said, and started at a gallop down the hill.

I watched him a bit, looked at the Xhosas, then followed. Halfway down the hill, I looked back. The Xhosas were gone.

I didn't like this at all. It was a dislike I'd developed out in Nebraska and the Dakotas, up in Montana. Riding through empty country, not a soul in sight, then the enemy, right where, a moment before, there had been nobody.

There were no tracks in the empty riverbed. I rode up it a ways, then down it. Yancey waited on the other side, his little horse wheeling, he himself impatient to move on.

Riding up to him, I said, "Yancey, this is just the kind of situation those boys in the Twenty-fourth got into. Nobody there, then every Zulu in the world. This is their country. They know how to hide in it."

"You want to go back, go back," he said, wheeling his horse around and starting up the far ridge.

I followed.

Halfway up the ridge, we spotted them, two men outlined against the sky, watching us from the top of the ridge.

"There!" Yancey shouted. "See them?"

"Yancey!"

But he was spurring his little pony now, right toward the two fellows atop the ridge, who stood a moment, then disappeared on the other side.

I pushed my pony, hard, catching up with Yancey as he neared the top of the ridge.

"Stop!" I shouted. "Turn back!"

But nothing was going to stop the quirky little leftenant. He'd seen the prize and he was going for it.

I would have turned. I should have turned. Every

instinct told me that the other side of that ridge was death and sorrow. But Yancey wouldn't stop, and I couldn't let him go it alone.

Then we were there, and down a way, to the left, I saw the two men, running down the hill. And beyond them, in the valley below, were thousands upon thousands of Zulus.

"My God," Yancey said.

They were a great black mass, moving south, two miles, maybe three away, filling the valley from one end to the other.

"It's a bloody army," Yancey said.

"Yancey," I said. "Let's go."

And we went, like the wind.

———

Yancey reported to his captain. I went in search of Briarmoore and a drink.

It was Bombay gin, warm and bitter, but it passed my gullet as easy as water.

"And you saw 'em?" Briarmoore asked.

"Yeah," I said.

We were sitting in his tent, he on one cot, I on another. I held the gin bottle in my left hand and used a kerchief with my right to wipe my face. I took another swig of the gin and handed the bottle back to Briarmoore.

Briarmoore asked, "How far from here?"

"An hour's ride, a little more."

"A lot of them."

"I tried to count," I said, "but there were too many. They filled the valley, one end to the other, a good four miles."

"Bloody rot."

"Yeah," I said.

And Briarmoore took a hit off the gin bottle.

## VIII.

THE BOYS looked fine in their blue coats. It was the distinctive uniform of the King's Guard, setting them apart from the standard red coats of the British Army. The King's Guards' boys did indeed look grand with their shiny white helmets and their Martinis shouldered. They marched, three hundred strong, at the back of the column, just ahead of the supply wagons. Yancey and I rode alongside his company on the little ponies, walking them to keep abreast of the marching infantry.

"Ain't it swell?" Yancey said to me.

"Yes," I said, "swell."

Briarmoore walked alongside his platoon.

We were bound for a Zulu stronghold at Hlobane Mountain to mount a diversionary attack, with Sir Evelyn Wood at the head of the two-mile-long column. Lord

Chelmsford, meanwhile, was leading another column to the south for the main attack to relieve British troops who had been under siege at Eshowe for thee months.

It was early morning, March 27, and we were headed in the very direction Yancey and I had covered weeks before. As we moved, I couldn't help but think of the massive Zulu force we had encountered. At a briefing the evening before, Colonel Napejack had assured all the officers of the Guard that the main Zulu force was at Eshowe. There would be, no doubt, a formidable foe at Hlobane, but it was only a holding party, and he was confident that we had sufficient force to accomplish our mission. We simply were to take Hlobane Mountain, kill as many Zulus as we could, and serve as a blocking force against the main Zulu army should it attempt to retreat north from Eshowe.

I could understand why Yancey thought things were swell. There is an excitement when men march into battle. I'd felt it before, back on the plains in Kansas and the Dakotas. But I doubt there was a man in that column, including Yancey, who wasn't thinking of Isandlwana. I know I was.

We saw Hlobane Mountain a long time before we got there. And it wasn't much of a mountain, more a good-sized hill. But whoever was atop it had plenty of warning. From up there, one could probably see to the curve in the earth.

The column encamped along a dry wash along which were a few abandoned mud huts, a town, actually, called

Khambula. We were but an hour's march from the base of Hlobane. The plan, I surmised, was to dig in for the night, get organized, and attack in the morning.

At supper, I sat with Briarmoore. Yancey was off to an officers' meeting. There was a double watch set out, and we could see fires atop Hlobane, a lot of fires. Briarmoore's read of that was that there were either a lot of wogs up there or a lot of fires.

I was eating some tinned beef when the captain walked up. He was the one who had briefed Yancey and me on our patrol.

Briarmoore and I both stood up.

"Crofton," the captain said.

"Sir."

"About that rifle."

"Sir?"

"It's not becoming for an officer to carry a rifle. Do you have a side arm?"

"Yes, sir."

"Suffice with that."

And he turned and walked away.

I looked at Briarmoore.

"Who is that?" I asked.

"He's a cunt," Briarmoore said.

Yancey returned from the officers' meeting a little before nine. He had a bright, though concerned, look on his face.

"In the morning," he said, squatting down near our

fire. "An artillery bombardment commencing at seven, then we go up at eight. We'll have the right flank."

Briarmoore asked, "Do they know what's up there?"

"Zulu," Yancey said. "Don't know how many."

Briarmoore looked at the fire. So did Yancey and I.

———

The attack began well enough. We were spread out in a line about a mile long, and each part of the line kicked off at exactly eight. There had been some movement atop the mountain, and the twelve-pounders had been accurate with their fire at the summit, kicking up a lot of smoke and dust. There hadn't been any return fire. Yancey's platoon had the middle of our right flank movement, and he walked slightly ahead of the men. I walked beside him. Contrary to the captain's wishes, I was carrying my rifle. I had the Colt pistol tucked inside my tunic, extra bullets for the rifle in cartridge boxes at my belt, bullets for the pistol in my pants pocket.

Yancey spoke. "I don't see anything. Do you?"

"Rocks."

"Do you suppose they're all dead up there?"

We had gone a half mile. To my left, I could see the rest of the line, everybody staying even, everybody quiet, rifles at ready. It was the stillness that was most evident. The crack of the twelve-pounders had left everyone a bit jumpy, but now there was only the sound of men's feet, an uneven cadence as they pushed up the grassy incline.

Briarmoore came up behind Yancey and me. Yancey turned to him.

"Do you think they're all dead up there?" Yancey asked Briarmoore.

"No, sir."

"You'd think they'd shoot or throw rocks or arrows or something," Yancey said.

A half mile from the summit, everybody's nerves were beginning to fray, and the going was rough now, a semivertical incline, men gasping for breath, grasping for a handhold, and always their eyes pinned to the summit, where, for the life of me, I could see no movement. The attacking line was ragged now, those in the center formation falling behind because of the roughness of the terrain, the far left formation split and scattered by outcroppings and precipitate inclines. We on the right were actually out ahead a good two hundred yards.

I was looking down, seeking a toehold, when I heard Yancey.

"Oh, God."

I looked up. The entire rim of the summit was covered with Zulus, black against the sky. There were thousands of them.

Then they came down, an avalanche of men, gaining in speed as they came.

Yancey pushed by me. "Down there," he said, gesturing. "That flat piece of ground. We'll form up there. Briarmoore!"

I scrambled backwards, not taking my eye off the Zulus, who were maybe two hundred yards away and coming fast.

"Form on the leftenant! Form on the leftenant!" I could hear Briarmoore's voice. But then it was drowned out by the shrill, almost hornetlike, sound of thousands of voices, the Zulus screaming as they came.

I got to the flat area, where Yancey was pushing men into line. I don't know how many men were there, maybe twenty, but Yancey got them into a firing line, and when the Zulus began to clamber down the rocks we'd all just left, Yancey gave the order to fire.

At first the fire from the Martinis was spotted, but it grew in intensity until it began to sound like corn popping, men firing quickly, levering out the spent cartridge, loading, firing again. And I was firing too, feeling the heavy recoil of the rifle against my shoulder, reloading, sighting, firing again. The Zulus began to fall. The outcropping they had to climb down had slowed them, and now both Yancey and Briarmoore were directing fire.

More of the boys joined us, Briarmoore pushing them into position, Yancey giving orders, stopping every so often to aim and fire his pistol, the lads calm, though all about us the world seemed to be spinning. I dared not look left or right, only to the front, pushing in a cartridge, drawing back the hammer, lifting the heavy gun, finding a man, pulling the trigger.

Then there was a lull, our front clear. I looked, left, right, to the rear.

"Yancey," I moved quickly to his side. "They're getting behind us."

He looked.

"Christ," he said.

All down the line, it was giving away, red coats being engulfed by a sea of black. Far away on the left, I could see white helmets going down, red coats falling back.

"We've got to fall back, Yancey."

"Briarmoore!"

"Sir."

"We're moving back down, a hundred yards." Yancey was looking to our rear. "To that clump of rocks. See it?"

"Yes, sir."

"Take half the men. We'll provide cover."

"Sir, yes, sir!"

I stayed with Yancey. We were directing fire now to both our left and our right. There were maybe thirty of us, and Briarmoore led half of them back, to the rocks, while the rest of us stayed, laying out suppressing fire to cover Briarmoore's movement.

Then, from the outcropping in front of us, a hundred or more Zulus jumped, didn't climb, but jumped, a good twenty feet to the ground, hit, rolled, came up, spears in hand, and charged.

They were on us before we hardly knew they were there, crashing into our small line, their short spears jabbing, their voices shrill with rage. I killed one with the rifle not ten feet from me, then dropped the rifle and drew my pistol from my tunic. The man standing next to me went down, a Zulu having driven a spear into his chest, and I shot the Zulu in the side of the head, two feet from me, the blood from his wound splattering onto my face. To my left I saw another, and I dodged his spear thrust, putting my pistol tight against his big brown stomach and pulling the trigger. He had a wide-eyed look of horror as the round exploded through him.

"Back! Back!" I heard Yancey's voice, ragged with excitement.

I grabbed the fat man's spear off the ground and used it to fend off two more attackers, shooting them both at five feet, then I was running with what was left of our little group, five, six, Yancey the last to come, not running exactly, but walking very fast, then stopping to turn and shoot with his pistol.

Briarmoore's men now gave us covering fire, and four men and I made it to the cover of the fallback position. Yancey came last, looking over his shoulder.

Briarmoore heard it first, a bugle call, recall.

"You hear it, sir?" he asked Yancey. "Recall."

"Thank God," Yancey said. "We'll go down, Briarmoore, but we're not going to run. We'll go down, five, ten men at a time, cover, and fall back. You understand?"

"Yes, sir."

"Crofton?"

"Yes?"

Yancey looked at me. "You go with Briarmoore."

"I'll stay with you, Yancey."

He smiled, then turned to the ten or so men still with him. "Put those bayonets on, boys. We're going to cut our way home."

And that's what we did. First Briarmoore's bunch, then Yancey's bunch, shoot, thrust, run, mayhem and madness, sweat and gasp, the noise deafening, and then more of the same, minutes really, which seemed like hours, until, finally, almost unbelievably, we were on flat ground, the Zulu not with us, rifles firing, the twelve-pounders cracking.

We collapsed on the yellow grass.

I had a metal, coppery taste in my mouth, and my breath came in great spasms of gasp, sweat burned my eyes, and I could feel my heart leaping inside my chest.

"Black hearts! Bitches! Bloody fuckers!"

I looked up. Briarmoore was up on one knee, his eyes fixed on the ground we'd just come from.

"They're killing the wounded," he said, his voice venomous with rage.

And he was up, a rifle with bayonet in his hands, and off.

I looked, and sure enough, fifty yards out, the ground was littered with men in blue, and the Zulus were clubbing and stabbing them. I got up, ejecting shells from my pistol as I ran, reaching into my pocket, loading, then, as I drew close to the slaughter, firing, one, two, three quick shots, three men down, then three more, and another three down.

I was behind Briarmoore. He had slashed two Zulus with the bayonet, leaving them bleeding on the ground, and had driven away a small band above one wounded soldier. Briarmoore pulled the man to his feet, literally lifted him up with one hand, the rifle in his other hand, the bayonet point threatening.

I raced to his side, reloading my pistol, then firing as Briarmoore dragged the man back to safety. Minutes later, Briarmoore returned, going for another downed Guardsman as I went with him. We each got a man then, both of us pulling the wounded to their feet, or dragging them by their arms. Oddly, several Zulus just stood and watched us, smiling, grinning, but others came at us, and several times Briarmoore and I had to drop the men we carried to fight.

I was out of bullets for the Colt, but I'd picked up one of the spears, and I used it to jab and thrust, stabbing one man, then another. Then Briarmoore and I were back to our rescue, grabbing the wounded English soldiers and dragging them back.

We went up, back, up, back. I lost count of the trips, but finally we went back one last time, the last time for Briarmoore. A dozen Zulus rushed him. He killed the first two, but the rest all got to him, ripping his body with their spears. I rushed them, killing one with a spear thrust into his back, then pulling it out, bringing out muscle and flesh, to hit another man, full in the face, the spear point going through the man's eye. And then I heard gunfire, and the Zulus began to drop or run.

I knelt down beside Briarmoore. He was dead. His body was jagged with wounds.

Five of the lads came up beside me and knelt and fired into the retreating Zulus.

I picked Briarmoore up and carried him back.

———

We'd suffered a terrible defeat. Colonel Woods got what was left of his force organized at Khambula, a half-mile line of defense, the big guns behind to provide fire support. The Zulus had exhausted themselves in their attack and waited now, up at the base of Hlobane, out of range. As the sun went down, I saw hundreds of bodies out on the plain before Khambula. All night we waited, knowing that, come dawn, the Zulus would attack.

———

Yancey was killed before the attack began. A single bullet, fired from a discarded rifle, by a man who probably didn't know how to reload it, fired out of the mist that shrouded the base of Hloblane Mountain, three hundred yards out, a lucky shot.

It hit Yancey in the chest, the big .45 caliber round going clear through, leaving a gaping hole in Yancey's back.

I held him and tried at first to stop the bleeding, but I knew it didn't matter. I knew nothing would save him. He looked up at me, his pale blue eyes watery, but no fear on his face.

"I guess I won't be winning the Victoria Cross," he said, then he died.

Some of the boys gathered around, looking down at Yancey. Several removed their helmets.

I sent one of them down the line to find the captain, to tell him what had happened. We moved Yancey's body back a ways and covered it with a blanket. Ten minutes later, the runner I had dispatched returned.

"You're to take the company," the runner told me.

"What?"

"That's what the captain told me. There aren't any more officers."

Sixty men, sixty frightened men, mostly boys, none of them as old as me, tired, cold, scared out of their wits.

I pulled two out of the line, brought them back to where the runner stood.

"You three," I said to them. "All you're to do is get bullets. Go back to the supply wagons. Get as many as you can. And bring them back to the line. Pass them out to those shooting. Keep moving, up and down the line. And rifles. Get as many rifles as you can. And water, canteens, buckets. Get as much of that as you can. Bring it up and keep going back for more. Keep us supplied, bullets and water. Do you understand?"

They all three nodded.

"Go," I said.

Then I turned to the line, walked up to the left side, and moved down it, tapping each fifth man.

"Start firing when I give the command, and keep firing. I'll get as much ammunition to you as I can, water too. If the rifle barrels get too hot, put water on them. If you don't have water, piss on them. But keep firing. We don't want them to get within fifty feet of us."

We were on flat land, not an iota of cover. The men knelt in firing positions. And out in front of us, mist, fog, Hlobane rising above it like an immense tombstone.

The Zulus came out of the mist, hundreds of them, their bodies glistening in the pale light. They made a grand charge, not even attempting to flank us but coming right at us, our little half-mile line bristling with rifles.

The twelve-pounders opened up first, sending shot and shell into the advancing ranks, knocking them down a half dozen at a time, and when they were a hundred yards out, I gave the order to fire, and all along our line the Martinis began to crack, the rate of fire increasing until it was one long, continuous roar.

I walked behind the men as they fired.

"Pick a target. Try for the body mass, the chest. Pick a target, boys. Don't shoot unless you have a target."

They came on, the Zulus, coming straight into the withering fire, falling by the score, but never hesitating, their shields made of animal skins doing them no good at all.

I had a rifle, and I fired too, not often, maybe every twenty steps, and once I saw a man I hit go down and the man behind him fall, the bullet having gone through the first to hit the second.

"Steady, boys. Steady. Find a target. Shoot at a target."

The lads I'd sent back for bullets came back with boxes of them, and they pulled them along behind the firing lines, soldiers reaching back to take handfuls and dropping them on the grass, to reach down, pick one up, jam it into the rifle, cock, and fire.

Finally, the Zulu attack faltered, and slowly they began to fall back, leaving scores of dead warriors on the field.

A cheer went up, up and down the line, Brits waving their helmets, cursing, praising God, jubilant.

Until the Zulus came again, more ferocious this time, angered by their failure, coming full tilt, by the hundreds, still.

"Volley fire, men!" I yelled. "In pairs. Fire after the man on your left has fired. Fire in turn. Quickly! Quickly, now!"

Oh, the boys were good. These Guardsmen were wonderfully disciplined, firing and loading in turn, keeping

CROFTON'S FIRE

a constant curtain of lead out in front of our position, knocking down Zulu by the score.

And on it went, a slaughter really, guns against spears, all through the morning and well into the afternoon. The Zulus breached our line only once, at the far right, and I went there with Yancey's pistol and my three ammunition bearers, and after a quarter-hour fight, bayonet and pistol against spear, we drove the Zulus back, losing ourselves a half-dozen men.

By midafternoon, I'd lost count of the assaults. And in front of us there were too many dead Zulus to count. Several of my boys' rifles had grown too hot, the barrels exploding, the rounds impacting back into the faces of the shooters. Water was scarce. Men were exhausted. Some simply dropped, from the heat, from the stress.

By late afternoon, the Zulu charges grew more and more feeble, and by evening, the battle was over, the Zulus moving back up Hlobane, the fight gone out of them.

In the quiet, exhausted silence, I counted my losses. I had twelve dead, twenty wounded.

One of the boys, I swear, he couldn't have been more than eighteen, asked me, "Did we win?"

I patted his shoulder, tried to smile. "We're still alive," I said.

He looked down at the ground and didn't say a word.

I went back to where Yancey's body lay. The blanket had been blown back and his face was revealed, his eyes closed, his skin white and stretched. But the look was one of calm—peaceful even. I sat down next to him. I was sitting there when darkness came.

———

The rains came. The weather turned cold. Through April and May, I moved when the Guards moved, sleeping on wet ground, eating cold food. Morale plummeted. We all experienced what the French call *cafard*, war weariness. I no longer had a command but had reverted to my original role, an observer. The leftenant who took over the platoon was an older man, not given to much talking.

There were a few more engagements, nasty, quick little fights that left the men tired and hollow. There was, I noticed, a kind of detachment, a dullness of mind that rendered us feeling impotent. It was as if we were all asleep, particularly when we were awake.

The Zulus were losing. We were all certain of that. They were hardly ever taken prisoner, but the few that were captured were dissolute and blemished, empty, tired men to whom death would probably seem a reprieve. There was talk of one last thrust, toward the Zulu capital of Ulundi, where the last battle would be fought.

In mid-June, I was summoned by Colonel Napejack, the regimental commander.

It was late evening, dark already, and the colonel's tent

was lighted by a single lantern. Colonel Napejack sat behind a folding table as I entered. The stiffness was gone from him, I could see that. He looked as tired as I was.

"Sir."

I stood before him, at attention.

"Sit, please," he said, nodding toward a stool in front of his table.

There was a moment or two of silence after I sat, the colonel simply staring down at the table. Finally, he spoke.

"There is no need for you to continue with us, Lieutenant," he said. "I imagine you would like to go home."

"Yes," I said, "I would."

"I'll make the arrangements."

"Sir?" The colonel looked at me. "I'll stay until it's over," I said.

Again the silence, until Napejack spoke. "You're sure?"

"Yes, sir."

Again the silence. He did not take his eyes off of me. Then: "Very well."

Then there was Ulundi, the last battle, Lord Chelmsford going in for the kill.

———

At Ulundi, the British brought to bear all the technological power of empire. In addition to a bevy of twelve-pound cannon, they introduced Gatling guns, a squadron of them. They were the 1877 Bulldog model, a five-barrel, .45 caliber weapon with a forty-round magazine feed. They were either mounted on a light cavalry cart or on a tripod and fired by a rear-mounted hand crank. They had a phenomenal rate of fire, a thousand rounds per minute.

The King's Guard were given a peripheral role in the final attack on Ulundi, a far-right flanking position, the thrust of the attack given to Chelmsford's own regiments at the center. The immense British column had reached Ulundi by the end of June. The weather was clear, the ground dry. Chelmsford had had overall command of the 24th back in January at Isandlwana, and he did not intend to make another mistake at Ulundi. From his headquarters on down, the unspoken command was total annihilation. There would be few prisoners taken.

I sensed this bloodlust in the few meetings our platoon had with senior officers. I sensed it, too, in the senior leftenant commanding the platoon. He was a quiet, sullen man, and when he outlined the plan for attack with platoon leaders, he left no doubt that our duty was to kill as many Zulus as possible, regardless of circumstance.

The attack began on the morning of July 4, and it was slaughter.

The Zulus, defending their home capital, came out with whatever zeal they could muster, and between the cannon and the Gatlings, they were killed by the hundreds. On our end of the British line, the men in the Guard did their share of killing. But I didn't. I held fire, but when I had to shoot, I shot for legs or feet. In my heart, I had no intention whatsoever of killing another black man.

It was a pitiful day, an ugly day, and by late afternoon, whatever was left of the Zulu nation had had enough. There were entreaties for a cease-fire, ignored by the British, then just as darkness began to fall, the Zulus mounted one final, feeble attack, only to be lethally repulsed. And as they retreated, the murder began.

British cavalrymen rode them down, killing them indiscriminately, with swords, spears, pistols. From my position on the far right, I saw one fellow wielding a cricket bat, riding hard upon running men, then whacking them in the head with the bat, splitting their skulls and sending them rolling. It took all the discipline I could muster not to shoot the man. I did raise my rifle, but fortunately, or unfortunately, however it might have been, he rode out of sight before I could decide to kill him or not.

At dark, British infantry moved into Ulundi and torched the town.

IX.

*August 14, 1879*
*Dear Mother,*
*I'm on a ship. I don't know the name of it. I never looked. No one ever told me. There are a couple*

*of hundred other men with me. All of them are wounded. I'm not wounded. I just hitched a ride. We're bound for London, should get there in about a week. From London I hope to ship home. I'm told there is quite a bit of crossing this time of year, so I shouldn't have any trouble finding a ship. I can hardly wait to see Louise and the babies.*

*I was in two battles in March, one at a place called Hlobane and one the next day at Khambula. In June I was involved in a big push toward Ulundi, the Zulu capital, and then there was a horribly big battle there July 4. There was much killing.*

*We've been at sea for five days. Someone dies every day, sometimes several. There are services each evening, and the dead men are dropped into the sea. They can't keep them on board. I help in the best way I can. There is so much suffering here. I read to some of the men, write letters for some of them. I try to find tobacco. Gangrene is the mortal danger here. The stench is awful. Some of the fellows know when their time has come and they asked me to fix them, to comb their hair.*

*They're all lower-class fellows, enlisted men. The officers were shipped earlier, on another ship. These lads are common. Some can read, some can't. They're almost all brave. Though some—no, most, I'd say—are scared of dying. There are no chaplains, no priests.*

*The ones who talk about it, I talk about it with them. Death seems so common to us now. I was talking to an orderly this afternoon, and he says the surgeons estimate we'll lose twenty percent before we get to England, maybe more. The screaming is what's worst. Sometimes it goes on all night.*

*War is a strange thing. The time I was here, down in Natal and over in Zulu country, it was an uncanny mixture of good and bad. I made some great friends, a sergeant named Briarmoore, a leftenant named Yancey. They were with the 44th King's Guard, the regiment I was assigned to. Oh, I had some fine times with those boys. They're both dead.*

*It's so hot. I must take water to the men.*

*Your son,*

*Michael*

## X.

LOUISE WAS all life and wonder and joy. She was light and heat and touch.

"It was a dream. It was a dream, Michael. There, now. There."

And her arms were around me in the still darkness, as my heart, galloping and wild, slowed, slowed.

"There, there."

Her hand upon my head, touching my face, the warmth of her breasts, full now with milk for the new child.

"I'm . . . I'm sorry."

"Shhhh. It's all right, baby. It's all right."

"I . . ."

"Sleep. Just lay back. Sleep, Michael, my Michael."

I fell back upon the pillow, her hand against my head, her lips brushing my cheek.

God is merciful. God is love.

"You are home," she said.

---

Cynthia Marie Crofton was a month old, all bubble and bliss, dark hair that seemed to lighten each day and dark eyes that got bluer each day.

I lay with her, September sunlight sliding lazily through the window onto the bed. She lay on her back, her head propped up on a pillow and I beside her. I took her chubby fingers in my hand as she kicked her legs, her other hand flailing the air.

She had come easily, her mother said, born in this very bed, two Negro midwives in attendance, church women. Louise had cried only because I wasn't there.

But I was there now, for my wife, for my son, for my thank-you-God precious daughter.

---

I had come from Liverpool to Baltimore. So I had not visited my parents, though Louise said they'd come to Washington when Cynthia Marie was born, had stayed, my father a week, my mother two weeks. They'd all worried about me.

But now I was home, with only dreams in my kit, bad dreams of death and flame and fear.

And duty.

"I'll have to report," I said to Louise over morning coffee.

"Yes."

Darien sat in my lap, little short pants on and no shirt. He was still sleepy and nodded against my chest.

I reached over the table, put my hand on Louise's.

"Your dreams," she said, "you've had one almost every night."

"They'll go," I said. "I'll dream them away."

"Was it so terrible?"

I looked at her.

"It's always terrible," I said. "You know."

"I was so afraid," she said.

"Me, too," I said, and smiled.

I put on my best uniform, the one I'd left behind, and went to the War Department. I asked for Colonel Samuelson. An orderly took me to an office at the back of the building. It was early, a little after eight. The walk down 17th Street had seemed unreal to me, that things should be so normal, men in hats, horse-drawn carriages passing by, the White House over there, all solemn and still.

"Lieutenant," Samuelson said, meeting me at his office door.

"Sir."

I started to salute, but he took my hand to shake instead.

"Come in, come in."

As I stepped into his office, Samuelson said to the orderly, "Get Sergeant Willis, please." Then, to me: "Please, Lieutenant, sit."

He pointed to a chair across from his desk, then went around behind the desk and seated himself.

"You are well?" he asked.

"Yes, sir."

"No fever, any of those unpleasant African things?"

"No, sir, I'm fine."

There was a knock at the door.

"Come," Samuelson said.

A sergeant came into the room. He carried a writing tablet.

Samuelson said, "This is Sergeant Willis. He's a transcriptionist. He'll be taking notes."

Willis took a chair against the wall.

"Now," Samuelson said, "the war."

"It was short," I said.

"Yes, it was, wasn't it."

I gave my report. I was versed enough in military jargon to outline basic strategies, to comment on tactics that had worked and on those that hadn't worked. I spoke of transport, supply depositions, fodder for animals, footwear, and food. In a half hour, I had given Samuelson, and Willis, an adequate history and analysis of the British campaign against the Zulus, with the right details that our military planners would need should we face a situation similar to that faced by the British, or should we face the British.

"Excellent," Samuelson said when I'd finished. "Now, what have you not told us?"

"Sir?"

"Your impression, your gut feeling. You were in the thick of it. How did the Brits do?"

"They slaughtered," I said. "At the end, at Ulundi, they murdered."

Samuelson looked blank. I glanced at the sergeant. He looked even more blank than the colonel.

"Can you explain that?" Samuelson asked.

"They took revenge for Isandlwana. They had no intention of allowing any Zulus to escape. They used cannon and Gatling guns, and when the Zulus quit, they chased them down and killed them with swords and spears and cricket bats. If it hadn't gotten dark, they would have killed them all."

"The enlisted men."

"The officers, too. Nobody tried to stop it."

Samuelson picked up a pencil from his desk and twisted it between his fingers.

"It was an unusual situation," he said. "Men far from home, afraid. You yourself said the Zulus were fierce warriors."

I didn't say anything.

Samuelson went on: "General Sherman will want to know about that rifle."

"Very effective," I said. "That forty-five caliber bullet does an enormous amount of damage. On several occasions, I saw it go through one man and kill another behind him. The rifle is easily maintained. I don't recall one jamming or misfiring."

We talked a bit more. Samuelson was interested in the Gatling guns. And he was curious about the command structure. He asked about the political situation surrounding the war, but I didn't know much about that. I said only that the British had an empire and they intended to keep it.

Samuelson dismissed Sergeant Willis.

When the colonel and I were alone in the room, he said, "It was bad, wasn't it?"

"Yes, sir, it was."

"White against black," he said. "Morality gets lost in something like that."

He turned from me, looked out the window.

"You made friends among the Brits?" he asked.

"Yes, sir."

"And?"

"They got killed."

He opened the drawer of his desk, took out a small black box, then said to me, "Your wife had a baby."

"Yes, sir, a little girl."

"This might help, then," he said, pushing the box across his desk to me. "You've been promoted. You're a captain now, an extra twenty-five dollars a month." I looked at the box. "Open it," he said.

I reached for it, pushed open the lid. Inside were two sets of gold captain's bars.

"Thank you, sir."

"I've also been authorized to give you a choice about assignment."

"A choice, sir?"

"Within reason."

"I don't understand," I said.

"You'll be moving out of Washington. Where would you like to go?"

I didn't know what to say. It didn't seem to me that I'd ever had a choice as far as the Army was concerned. And for just an instant, I thought of the 7th Cavalry, of Fort Riley and the plains and the fall out there, the high clouds and the blue sky and the grass turning brown and gold.

"West Point, sir," I said. "I'd like to teach there."

Samuelson smiled. "I'll see what I can do."

I stood up and saluted. He returned the salute.

As I turned to leave, Samuelson said, "Captain?"

I turned to look at him.

"It might be best," he said, "if you didn't mention that the British murdered anyone."

We left Washington on September 25. We hoped for a new life in my old one. I had hoped, coming home from England, that I would study war no more, but I knew, as our train traveled north, that its study would occupy me for years to come.

# Four

## I.

IF MY RETURN to Providence with Louise had been a trip back in time, my return to West Point was, too, but on a different plain. Providence had been my childhood home, the ground in which all of my emotional life had been sown. West Point was spirit, for it was there that I had learned of higher things, those things that transcend emotion. On the boat up the Hudson, as we neared the last bend around which West Point could be seen, I felt a rush of excitement. And when we made the last turn of the bend and I saw the Academy, I felt much as a Moslem with Mecca in sight.

"There," I said to Darien, whom I held in my arms. He was dressed, innocuously, in a little sailor suit. "See? That's West Point, up there, on that high bluff."

"Wa-ter," he said.

"Do you see?" I asked Louise.

"It's beautiful," she said.

And indeed it was, in the New York Indian summer, the river shining in the sun, the air crystal clear in the golden afternoon light. The trees still held their green, but it was that dark, full green of late summer, the last vibrant green before death and fall.

The boat, a small tourist steamer, puffed ashore, putting in at a heavy wooden dock below the Academy. Two men in blue shirts and black trousers caught the tie ropes and pulled the small vessel against the planking.

There were maybe a dozen people aboard, most bound for Albany, and my family and I were the only ones to disembark. Once we were up on the dock, the ropes were let loose, the little steamer was free, and it pushed back out into the river.

We had only two bags, which I handled, and a small one that Louise held in one hand, Cynthia Marie in her other arm. Darien stood silently, a bit intimidated by the two dock men, swarthy fellows with big beards and tanned arms and faces.

"Welcome, Cap'n," one of them said to me.

"Sir," I said.

"Need me to tote them bags?"

"Thank you, no," I said.

It was a steep climb, up a series of stairs, to the ground above. Little Darien had to negotiate each step, using his arms to reach up and then pull up, then repeat the process. He went first, Louise second, carrying Cynthia. I lagged behind, the two bags growing heavier with each new tier of stairs. We stopped several times, to rest, and to admire the view.

"So many trees," Louise said during one of our rests.

"Old trees," I said. "Some have been here forever."

"Daddy? Daddy?" I picked Darien up. He was pooped. Little dabs of sweat sprinkled his forehead.

Louise said, "You should have let that fellow carry the bags."

"During the war with England, the Revolutionary War," I said to Darien, to Louise, "they put a big chain across the river, right down there. An enormous chain. To keep British ships from going upriver."

Darien didn't seem too impressed.

"Colonel Thaddeus Kosciuszko designed the fortifications here, back during the Revolutionary War. He was Polish. It was a fine fort. Benedict Arnold sold it out. He was in command here, and he tried to give the British the information they needed to take it. It's history, so much history, here, all the time. Lee, Grant, Sherman, Longstreet. They climbed these stairs. Just like us."

"Leave the bags," Louise said.

"What?"

"Leave the bags. Carry Darien. When we get to the top, you can come back for them."

"Aye, Cap'n," I said.

At the top we were met by two scurrying cadets. They came down the hill in a run from the Academy proper, screeching to a halt as they met us. Seeing me, they stiffened to attention, threw salutes, and one of them spoke, in that particular plebeian tone, loud, succinct, and abrasive.

"Sir! Cadets Winslow and Harrington reporting!"

I saluted back. "At ease, boys. Reporting for what?"

"Sir!" said the same boy. "To aid the captain in his arrival at West Point, sir!"

Cynthia Marie started to cry. The boy's harsh voice frightened her.

"Ease it down a notch, son," I said. "Now, which of you is Winslow and which of you is Harrington?"

"Cadet Winslow, sir!" said the speaker, his voice a bit lower now.

"Cadet Harrington, sir!" said the other boy.

They were both no more than eighteen. They wore the Academy gray, slacks and tunic, buttoned to the top. And they had on those silly little hats with the half-visor.

"Winslow," I said. "You go down these steps here and fetch the two bags. Harrington, you lead my family and me to our quarters."

"Yes, sir!" both boys said in unison.

And Winslow went running down the stairs.

"Ma'am," Harrington said to Louise, taking her bag. "If you will follow me."

And we started up the path to the buildings above.

Little Cynthia Marie stopped crying once we got moving.

Harrington led us to a small house, set in a row of such houses along a tree-lined street paved with old, rust-red brick. There was a small covered front porch to the house and a brick walk leading up to it.

"Faculty housing, sir," Harrington said. His voice had just a bit of brogue to it.

I asked, "Where are you from, Harrington?"

"Quincy, Massachusetts, sir."

"Irish?"

"Irish-American, sir, third generation."

"Well, that's fine." I gestured toward the house. "Let's take a look."

It was a fine house, finer than our little nest on M Street. It had a nice, big, but cozy living room, a dining area back of it, and a door to the kitchen. Off to the right were two bedrooms. And it was all furnished—sofa, chairs, beds, a bit worn and probably taken from a hotel somewhere, but comfortable and certainly usable. Windows were cut into each outside wall, and the kitchen had a pump handle at the sink and a nice, big woodstove.

I looked out the window above the kitchen sink and saw a small yard and a privy at the back.

"This will do," I said to Louise.

She was still holding Cynthia Marie, who was squirming now, wanting to be let down.

"It's nice," Louise said.

"Sir?"

I went back to the living room. Winslow was standing just inside the door, holding the two big suitcases. He was breathing heavily, and there was sweat on his forehead and upper lip.

"Just set them down, Mr. Winslow," I said.

And so he did.

Harrington moved to stand next to him.

Winslow asked, "Is there anything else the captain requires of us?"

"No, thank you for your help."

"Sir?" Winslow went on. "You are requested to attend Major Philburn when it is convenient, sir. He is located in the administration building. Can we direct you, sir?"

"I know where it is."

"Yes, sir."

"You're dismissed, boys. Thank you for your help."

"Sir, yes, sir," Winslow said, as he and Harrington again snapped to attention and threw two more quick salutes.

I answered their salutes, and they turned and left the house.

Behind me, Louise said, "Do they always act like that?"

I turned to her. "The cadets? Yes, I'm afraid they do."

Darien, who was standing near the sofa, looked at me and saluted, his little right hand hitting his hair.

———

We'd visited Providence, for three days, on our trip from Washington. My parents were quite taken with Cynthia Marie. Both Mother and Father had been overly attentive of me, Mother especially. She'd received the letter I'd mailed from London. They were glad, both of them, that I was to teach at West Point. It was, of course, an honor, but mostly I think they were relieved that I'd no longer be in harm's way.

Colonel Samuelson had been good as his word. I'd been notified by courier less than a week after my visit with the colonel that I'd been assigned to the faculty at West Point. Just what exactly I'd do there, what courses I'd teach, had been vague. I was only to report. Assignments would be made after that.

We arrived the last of September, the fall term already under way. I stayed with Louise for an hour, helping unpack and sort our few clothes and belongings. We had other paraphernalia to arrive, having been shipped overland from Washington, mostly household items and children's toys and such. Then, family ensconced, I left to report to Major Philburn.

The major, it turned out, was not in his office but was instead watching a baseball game, or so his elderly assistant, a slight woman with grayish white hair, informed me. I did not know where the baseball field was. There had been no baseball when I was at West Point. With directions, however, I found it, on a level field that served, on other occasions, as a firing range for the artillery.

A gaggle of cadets was there, and families, too. The players, all wearing ragamuffin clothing, littered the playing field like so many toy soldiers, in a broad and unrecognizable formation.

I asked a cadet, and he pointed out Philburn for me.

"Major Philburn?" I said, standing next to the man.

He turned, a slender man of medium height, goatee and sideburns, hair a light brown. He wore the uniform, his major's leaves upon his collar.

"I am Captain Crofton," I said, saluting.

The major didn't return the salute, but said instead, "A wonderful thing, baseball, and purely American. They'll tell you it's just a version of cricket, but it's not. Not at all. Cricket is such a prissy sport. This, though, the ball like a stone and thrown hard, is tough. It's a fast, aggressive game. We're organizing it in the spring."

"Yes, sir," I said.

"Do you play?"

"I'm afraid not, sir. I've never seen the game."

"It's big and getting bigger."

Apparently, someone did something exciting at that moment, because the crowd burst into cheers and applause.

The major looked to see. "A two-baser!" he crowed.

"Way to go, boys! Yes!" Then, turning to me: "We're play-ing a team from Yonkers, semiprofessional. Brawlers. Half of them are tanked. Do you know? There'll be a fight soon. Ah, it's a great game."

But duty called, and the major and I departed the scene.

Walking back to the campus, Philburn asked, "You've quartered with your family?"

"Yes, sir."

"Good. There are just some papers. You know the Army. We have to write you in or you will not exist."

"Yes, sir. Major, if I may ask, what is it exactly that I will be doing?"

"I have no idea," he said, perkily. "But I hope it's some-thing modern. Get us past that dusty old Civil War. My God, who wants to hear again about Pickett's charge?"

We walked a bit more.

"Have you met General Schofield?" Philburn asked. Schofield was the superintendent of West Point. "Wonder-ful man. Beat old John B. Hood down in Tennessee. Medal of Honor. Secretary of War under Johnson. A blessing to the Point, if I do say so. Modern. Yes, there's the feeling now. We must be modern. It's a new world, don't you think? A modern world."

"It's the weapons that are modern," I said.

"Yes, I daresay," Philburn said. "Let's get you on the payroll."

And we started again, toward the campus.

The dreams still came, but with less severity. Only occasionally did I wake, clawing at the air. The dreams now were less intense but more real. There were soldiers in the dreams, long lines of them, their white helmets stark against the blue-black African sky. And I could hear sounds in the dreams, the voices of sergeants, the drum of rain upon the tent roof, the chants of the Zulus as they taunted.

There were the dead. I still held Yancey. And I still carried Briarmoore through smoke and dust. A soldier next to me, his face slashed away. The black men I had killed, sometimes with my pistol, as they were right upon me. The looks in their deep-brown eyes as the bullet tore through their bodies. And the fields of them, at Khambula, at Ulundi. Hundreds and hundreds of bodies.

"You can't go through something like that and not have it affect you," I said.

Louise and I lay awake just at daylight, the two children sleeping, our little bedroom quiet. I'd come up from one of the dreams, and Louise now held me. It was a still morning, the light in the room just moving from black to gray.

"It's not natural," I went on. "It's outside the realm of anything we've been taught. There is no way one can prepare for it. It's this terrible slide backward, past knowledge, into a kind of horrendous past.

"The Zulus knew it. I think they knew it more than the whites. When they came at us, dying by the score, I thought, at first, that they were so incredibly brave. But later, I knew too. They had no thoughts, no emotions. You are hypnotized by the smoke, the fire, the noise. You lose all awareness but the one, the need to stay alive. You will do anything to stay alive. Anything."

I felt Louise's hand gently stroking my hair.

———

Truthfully, General Schofield didn't look like a Medal of Honor winner. Older, balding, plump, he looked like a man who might run a successful hardware store. But he was the superintendent of West Point, had fought and beaten Hood in Tennessee, and had negotiated the French out of Mexico. A major general, he had rank and experience, and as superintendent of West Point, he had the same status as Robert E. Lee, who had been the Point's superintendent when Schofield graduated from there in 1853.

My meeting with the superintendent was a formal affair, Philburn there, and two other ranking officers, a Colonel Parker and a Lt. Colonel Bierce.

Schofield introduced me to these men, then indicated I should take a seat before his desk.

It was my third morning at West Point. I had been informed of the interview with General Schofield the day before by a cadet sent from Philburn. I sat now, in my dress blues, rigid and hot in spite of it being a cool day, the windows to Schofield's office open to a friendly breeze off the Hudson.

"Captain," Schofield said from behind his massive desk. "We are glad to have you at West Point. You've received a positive recommendation from a number of sources."

I said, "I'm glad to be here, sir."

"Your family is settled?"

"Yes, sir."

"You graduated from West Point in 1874. Is that correct?"

"Yes, sir."

Schofield raised a handkerchief to his eyes, used it to rub them, then continued.

"We are effecting changes at West Point, Captain Crofton. We are eliminating some of the more undesirable practices. I do not personally believe that the young men in our charge respond positively to negative treatment. Do you understand?"

"Yes sir."

"Our duty is to prepare these boys to be officers in the United States Army. We are to help them, not hinder them. Discipline, of course, will remain in effect. As will obedience to orders. But harsh treatment, of any kind, will not be tolerated."

Glory be, I thought, remembering, in a quick flash, my own treatment at West Point, the scathing insults, the physical abuse, the foul practice of hazing. There were few kind words in my four years, the belief being then, a belief that I had subscribed to, that hard treatment made hard men.

"You are to be a mentor, Captain," General Schofield said. "As an experienced soldier from the field, you are to nurture these young men, to strengthen them with your support, your goodwill, and your patience."

"Yes, sir."

"If there are any . . . problems, you are to refer them to Colonel Parker." Schofield gestured toward the colonel, who sat to my right. "He is in charge of discipline here."

"Yes, sir."

There was a bit more talk, about dining room privileges, a request to attend chapel, and the offer of a horse. I was to have full access to the academy stable. Then, strangely, there was a kind of lull, after which General Schofield asked me if I had any questions. When I responded no, the interview was over. Everybody stood up, there was a cordial round of handshakes, we all saluted the general, and the occasion was over.

Afterward, I walked with Philburn across the quad.

"Captain Crofton," he said, "you did not inform me of your status."

"My status?"

"Are you by any chance related to General Sherman?"

"No."

We reached the dining hall, where Philburn was bound for lunch. I was going home to lunch with Louise and the kids.

"Major?" I asked.

He looked at me.

"What am I to do? No one has said anything of my duties."

"In due time, my boy," Philburn said. "In due time."

And he disappeared into the dining hall.

Louise thought I was being punished.

"Why would I be punished?" I asked over beans and rice, our lunch.

"Your Army," she said. "Who knows anything? They sent you and Sorensen off to Cuba, didn't they? With no idea of what you were to do? And why were you sent to Africa? What could possibly be the reason for that? And now they've moved you out of Washington. Why? Were you an embarrassment to them?"

"Louise," I said, "I had no idea you felt this way."

"Michael? Our baby was just born. Darien wasn't a day old. And they whisked you away. And you weren't even there for Cynthia Marie."

Whatever appetite I had for the rice and beans evaporated.

Cynthia Marie was coddling in Louise's lap, and Darien was sitting on a box on a chair, playing with his rice and beans.

"This is different, Louise," I said, quietly. "I won't be going anywhere now. West Point is not temporary. That's why I asked for it." I gestured with my hand. "This is our home. It's as permanent as the Army can be."

She looked at me, her face a pretty pout.

I smiled at her.

She looked at me some more, her eyes getting that oh-so-wonderful glint.

"Let's put the babies down for a nap," I said.

The glory of West Point on an autumn afternoon, the sun arching through the windows, the distant sound of boys marching, our babies asleep, the leafy, river smell of the tangy air, my darling wife pushing up against me, her wonderful body open to all the love and trust and hope that I had in me, our skin as white as the sheets on which we moved, in slow, warm, wet motion, and the gentle, wafting climb, first her, then me, to fall, from a high and bright distance, into each other's arms, and sleep.

"Daddy?"

I opened an eye. Darien stood next to the bed.

"Gotta pee-pee."

"Ah, yes," I said. "Good boy. Very good boy."

And in pants, barefoot, suspenders ajar, I walked my son across the velvety backyard to the privy, where he took a good and wholesome, masculine, stand-up pee.

When Darien and I returned to the kitchen, Louise met me there.

"There is a general in the living room," she whispered. She was wearing her housecoat, a strapping, floppy thing, and her hair was disheveled. She still had that loving look about her, but obviously she was embarrassed.

"A general?" I whispered back.

"He knocked," she said. "I went to the front door. I thought it was one of those cadets. Michael, I look a mess."

I reached down and kissed her cheek. "You look lovely," I said.

"Mama," Darien said. "I make pee-pee."

I slipped from the kitchen into the bedroom, and while I was tucking in my tunic, I heard my son.

"I make pee-pee."

There was a quivering silence, then the voice of a man.

"Well, that's wonderful, son."

General Schofield. Oh, my God.

"General, sir," I said, coming into the living room. Oh, Lord, I was wearing only socks. I'd forgotten my shoes.

Darien, wearing only a pair of short pants, was standing looking up at the general.

I started to salute, then I didn't. Should I salute in my own living room?

"Captain," said General Schofield. "I assume this is your son."

"Yes, sir," I said, scooping up the boy. "Will you have a seat, sir?"

I hustled Darien back to Louise in the kitchen. She took him and gave me one of those looks of calamity.

When I returned to the living room, General Schofield was seated on the sofa. He had removed his hat. But otherwise, he was the Medal of Honor general officer, sitting there in my living room like a lion in a chicken coop.

"Would you like something, sir? Coffee?"

"No, thank you. I am sorry to intrude like this on you, Captain. I should have sent notice."

"It's quite all right, sir."

I took a seat in the chair opposite the sofa.

Schofield cleared his throat, then said, "Well." I noticed for the first time that he was carrying a folder. "I have been in correspondence with General Sherman. I wanted you to be aware of what the general has written."

He opened the folder and handed me a letter.

The letter was handwritten and dated 18 September 1879.

*Dear General Schofield,*

*Captain Michael Crofton will be joining your command soon. I would most appreciate your finding a spot for him. He is an excellent officer and has done some outstanding work for me. I believe he wants to be a teacher.*

*You will find enclosed a copy of a letter sent to me by a Colonel Napejack of the 44th King's Guard. He commanded a regiment to which Captain Crofton had been assigned during the late conflict in southern Africa.*

*Captain Crofton is to be awarded the Victoria Cross, a rather high honor among the Brits.*

*Sincerely yours,*

*Wm. T. Sherman*

I looked up from reading. Schofield gestured for the letter, and when I handed it to him, he handed me another.

*7 Sept. 1879*
*General William T. Sherman*
*Commandant, U.S. Army*
*Subject: Lieutenant Michael Crofton*

*Dear General Sherman,*
    *I wish to inform you that Lieutenant Michael Crofton, U.S. Army, is to receive the Victoria Cross, Great Britain's highest military honor. Lt. Crofton is being cited for his actions with the 44th King's Guard at engagements against Zulu tribesmen at Hlobane and Khambula, March 28–29 of this year.*
    *At Hlobane, Lt. Crofton showed exemplary bravery in repeated forays into charging Zulu warriors to rescue wounded British soldiers. He did so at great personal risk. The following day at Khambula, Lt. Crofton assumed command of a company of Guardsmen when their commanding officer was killed. Against a force outnumbering them by at least ten to one, the company held the line and delivered disciplined fire against the enemy, resulting in a successful repulse.*

*Lt. Crofton is the first non–British national to receive the Victoria Cross.*

*Sincerely,*

*Jonathan Napejack*

*Regimental Commander*

*44th King's Guard*

I thought of Yancey, and for just a moment I felt tears welling up in my eyes.

"Quite an accomplishment, Captain," General Schofield said.

I handed Napejack's letter back to him.

The general then said, "There will be a ceremony, here at West Point. President Hayes will attend and present the award to you. General Sherman will be in attendance also. I believe, too, that the British Ambassador will be here. The date has yet to be arranged."

"General," I said, "I'm sorry about my boy."

He looked at me and said, "Making pee-pee? Why, Captain, that too is quite an accomplishment."

## II.

"THERE ARE those who deserve this more than me."

"I know, Michael, but they're giving it to you."

Louise and I lay awake that night, having pillow talk. It was unusually warm. We lay atop the covers.

"I don't know what it means," I said.

"You're a hero."

I thought a bit, then said, "I don't know what that means, either."

"How will this change things?" Louise asked.

"I'm not sure. I suppose it means I will stay on at West Point. For a while. I'll be their resident success story. Yancey, you remember I told you about Yancey? The little leftenant I shared a tent with? He called the Victoria Cross the boss. Said one's career was oiled—that's the word he used, oiled—if one won the V.C."

"So you can become a general?"

"I don't want to be a general."

Louise was quiet awhile, then asked, "What do they pay a general?"

There was a glow about me now. I wasn't completely aware of it, but in my daily dealings with colleagues, they apparently noticed it.

"I'm envious," Philburn said.

He and I stood before the administration building. It was a gray, drippy day, mist but no rain. Philburn had been put in charge of the ceremony.

"Don't be," I said.

"But I am, Captain. There are so few—how shall I put it? Rewards, yes. There are so few rewards in the Army. You've just gotten one, and I haven't."

Work would begin, as soon as the weather cleared, on a dais, to be made of wood, elevating the players, as Philburn termed them, above the masses. President Hayes, General Sherman, General Schofield, the British Ambassador, and, of course, I, would all be positioned up high, so the entire corps could see. There would be a band. Politicians would flock to the event, particularly New York politicians. And the press—ah yes, the press.

"Schofield may appear a kindly old grandfather," Philburn said, "but mark my word. He will milk this situation. You're the prize stallion in the stable now, Captain. Schofield will see to it that your picture is on the front page of every newspaper in the country. Along with the words 'West Point.' You are a publicity gold mine."

"Major?"

"Yes?"

"There's no way to avoid this?"

He smiled at me. "No," he said. "Duty, honor, country, sir."

I went down to the stables.

Even in the muck of the day, I was comfortable on horseback. And the horse was a good one, a big black who appreciated as much as I the opportunity to get out and about.

The weather was turning. This misty, gray day was the harbinger of winter, the first truly fall day. Out and away from the academy campus, I could at times see the river below and a length of the valley it formed. The green was splotched with color now, dull reds, rust colors, and the pale yellow green of leaves tinged with dying. In another two weeks, the Hudson Valley would be breathtaking in its color, full autumn an explosion of the more violent of colors, blood reds, wild yellows, and orange.

As I rode, at a canter, then a run, then a slow, cooling walk, I remembered my early years at this place, the seasons, each one distinct; and I remembered, too, that fall was best. There would be smoke from the burning leaves, columns and layers of it, as far as the eye could see, and that soft, burnt smell of it. The corps would be issued winter wear about now. The mornings would grow crisper, the nights perfect for sleeping.

The auspicious day was set for the third Saturday in October. Announcements were sent out. The press was notified. Louise and I bought clothes for the children.

Still I could not grasp the whole of it.

When I told this to Philburn, he suggested a speech.

"You'll have to give one, you know," he said.

We were in his office, the Monday before the ceremonial Saturday.

"A speech?" I said.

"Of course. Nothing long, mind you, but an acknowledgment of the honor, thanks to the Queen, that sort of thing."

"I can't give a speech."

"Of course you can. Thanks a lot, God save the Queen. There's your speech in a nutshell. Tell me, what was it like, those two days of battle?"

"What was it like?"

"Yes. The smoke and the roar and the general excitement."

"I was scared," I said, "scared to death."

Philburn looked at me, blankly.

The remainder of that week was agonizing. I could not concentrate. I rode every day, trying, I think, to outride the agony. When I was on the black, I was away from the moment. The animal required no speech. He responded to the rein, to the heel in his side, any command merely a movement.

As the horse and I traipsed across the country north and east of the academy, I was possessed of an incredible desire to keep on riding, up through the forest, in whatever direction I was headed, ride until dark, make camp, then set out again the next morning. There comes a time in every man's life, as McCallum would put it, to skedaddle.

But I didn't skedaddle, and the Friday night before the moment, I didn't sleep either.

"What's wrong?" Louise asked.

I was sitting on the edge of the bed in just my skivvies. It was early, early morning, dark and cold.

"I don't want this."

She moved across the bed, put her arms upon my shoulders, her body pressed against my back.

I said, "No one should be given an award for what I did. All that killing. It's mad."

## III.

SATURDAY MORNING rose up out of the Hudson River Valley brilliantly. It would be, much to my dismay, a glorious day. There was a hint of frost on the backyard as I made my way to the privy and back. The sky was a deep blue and the sunlight golden.

I couldn't eat. I had only coffee for breakfast.

Darien scooted around, animated by expectation. He didn't know exactly what was going on, but he knew it was something, and when Mama dressed him in his little corduroy suit, he grew even more excited.

Even Cynthia Marie seemed caught up in the clamor. Only three months old, she twisted and turned in my lap, gurgling with excitement. It took me an inordinately long time to pin her diaper.

And then Louise. She emerged from the bedroom in her blue dress, a wide white hat with a deep-blue ribbon tilted back on her head, looking very much like royalty, her blond hair radiant down and around her shoulders, her bright eyes twinkling.

"You look . . . wonderful," I said.

"You think so?"

"Oh yes. Extraordinary."

"Dress, Michael. Your uniform is laid out on the bed."

And so it was, a formal dress uniform, lent to me by the academy, twin gold captain bars temporarily stitched to the shoulders, pants with a gold stripe, the buttons gold-colored. There were white gloves, and, of all things, a sword. It was, of course, only a ceremonial sword, its edge blunted, but it had a fine ivory handle and a gold-colored hilt. The scabbard was deep, and dark leather.

I dressed slowly. The tunic was tight-fitting and the trousers a tad long. I felt silly when I buckled on the sword.

In the living room, my little family stood silently when I stepped out of the bedroom. Even Darien paused.

"My," Louise said.

"Do I look that stupid?" I asked.

Louise paused, then said, slowly, "You look . . . soldierly."

We walked to the administration building. I carried Darien. Louise carried Cynthia Marie.

The crowd was already building when we got there. The large wooden dais was set up at the head of the quad, just in front of the administration building, and there was a large, vacant area in front of it where the corps would assemble. On each side, civilians were gathering, men in dark suits, a sprinkling of women in dress and jacket. The sun was shining bright, not a cloud in the azure blue sky, not even a wind, just a small breeze coming up off the river. It wasn't cold. It wasn't hot. A perfect day. The flag on the pole behind the dais riffled only slightly.

Louise, the children, and I went into the administration building. In the great hall there, Philburn met us.

"Well," he said, all aglow in his own dress blues. "Look

at you. What a picture. A family West Point can be proud of. Mrs. Crofton, you look lovely."

And he took her hand, shaking it gently.

Then he shook my hand, more rigorously.

"Captain," he said, "this is your moment in the sun." He let go of my hand, looked at me curiously, then asked Louise, "Why does he look so glum?"

Louise said, "He's a pickle-pud."

"Ah," said Philburn.

Philburn took a folded piece of paper from inside his tunic, unfolded it, then looked up at us.

"The agenda," he said. "Colonel Bierce will welcome everyone to West Point, then introduce General Schofield. The superintendent will make a few remarks, then introduce President Hayes. The President will, of course, give a speech, after which he will introduce General Sherman. Sherman will make a few remarks, then introduce the British Ambassador, who will read the official citation accompanying the medal, then, Michael, you will come to the lectern and the President will present you with the Victoria Cross. It's on a ribbon, which he will drape around your neck. You will make a few remarks of your own, the President standing next to you. The military band will play the British national anthem, and that will be it. There will be a reception afterward at General Schofield's home. Any questions?"

When I didn't say anything, Philburn turned to Louise.

"There is seating for you and the children," he said to her, "just to the right of the dais, in the shade. Mrs. Schofield has asked that you be seated next to her. General Sherman's wife will be there, as will the wife of the British Ambassador. Unfortunately, the First Lady, Mrs. Hayes, could not come."

Philburn took a watch from his pocket.

"Well, shall we proceed?"

The presentation ceremony was to begin at noon. By eleven, a crowd had gathered. A little after eleven, Louise took the children to their seating beneath the trees, and I waited with Philburn in his office in the administration building.

Philburn was fluttery. He kept looking at his watch. At 11:30, he excused himself, and I was left alone in his office.

Try as I might, I couldn't escape thoughts of Yancey. It didn't seem fair that he was dead and I was receiving this medal. It should have been his. That day on the mountain, at Hlobane, Yancey kept his wits about him. The men in his company were panicked. I was panicked. It seemed to me that the whole Zulu nation had risen out of nowhere and were now upon us. But Yancey would not allow his men to run. He held them in check, and when the order came to retreat, Yancey's company did so in an orderly way.

That night when the fighting had ceased, I remembered sitting with Yancey. Then he was scared. He'd kept his fear hidden all day, but that night, he couldn't hold a cup steady enough to keep the tea in it. He trembled body and soul, but his men didn't see it. Only I saw it.

"We've got a problem."

I looked up. Philburn had come back into his office, a flustered look on his face.

"What?" I asked.

"Tilden men."

"Tilden men?"

The rancor of the Hayes-Tilden presidential election of 1876 had not dissipated, at least not in New York, Samuel J. Tilden's home state. That election had been chaotic, too close to call. Hayes had emerged the victor, due, many believed, to some clever political maneuvering, some if not all of it vaguely illegal.

The Republicans had claimed victory, but so did the Democrats, yet Hayes had been sworn in as President (by Grant, in the dead of night), not Tilden. Hayes claimed victory with an electoral vote majority of one. Subsequent tallies gave Tilden fifty-one percent of the popular vote.

"They've come up from the city," Philburn said. "A couple of hundred of them. They're carrying signs."

In the distance, I heard music. The West Point band was playing.

Sherman came walking into Philburn's office.

Without even thinking, I stood and snapped to attention.

"Major," Sherman said, "what are you doing about those hoodlums out there?"

Philburn had snapped to attention, too. "Sir," he said.

Sherman was dressed to the nines, his uniform creased and shiny, gold epaulets on his shoulders, a sash at his waist, and a sword too.

"Well?" he said, staring Philburn in the eye.

Philburn said, "I have consulted with Mr. Dryer, President Hayes's chief bodyguard. And I have wired the sheriffs in three adjoining counties. They are bringing deputies."

Sherman turned away from Philburn and slapped his left hand with the gloves he held in his right.

"A volley into them," he said. "Knock down a half dozen and we'd have no trouble from them the rest of the day." Then he looked at me. "Crofton." I saluted. He saluted back. "The Victoria Cross," Sherman said. "Aren't you the shine on the minnows."

Then he left the room.

Philburn pulled a handkerchief from his back pocket and wiped his face.

At 11:45, Philburn and I left his office and went outside to assume our positions on the dais. As we mounted it, the corps came marching in, four hundred strong, in tight formation, each cadet dressed in formal Academy gray. They were a splendid sight, their ranks precise, the band playing a martial air. It took them but ten minutes to fill the open space directly in front of the dais, all standing at attention, their ranks forming a perfect square, their regimental flags fluttering in the slight breeze.

At five minutes until twelve, General Schofield leading the way, President Hayes, General Sherman, and the British Ambassador to the United States mounted the dais.

I had, of course, seen President Hayes, on occasion, when I was stationed in Washington, but never this close. He passed right before me, full-bearded, wearing a heavy black coat, his dark hair long and combed. After he passed, I looked to Louise and saw her, and Darien and Cynthia Marie, sitting serenely in the shade of the trees. Louise waved at me, and I nodded my head at her.

Then the boos and the catcalls began. A large contingency of men, to the left of the dais and back a way, were yelling and chanting, some waving signs. One sign read, "Welcome Your Fraudlency," another, "Rutherfraud B. Damned," and several read simply, "Thief."

Here, almost three years after the election, in Tilden's home state, much of the anger and frustration felt by Democrats was being reignited.

The noise grew. Colonel Bierce took the lectern and tried to speak.

"Cadets, ladies and gentlemen, esteemed guests, welcome to West Point. We are here today—"

"Traitor!"

"Thief!"

"To hell with Hayes!"

Then an egg came arching through the air, splattering against the lectern.

Then, to the right, there came another hubbub. Loud voices, curses, snatches of song, and I saw maybe a hundred men entering the quad, rough men in work clothes, carrying ax handles and sticks and bottles.

"Oh, my God," Philburn muttered. He was sitting next to me. "Yonkers."

I leaned over to him. "What?"

"It's the ballplayers from Yonkers."

Sherman leaned forward in his chair, his eyes blazing, and snapped a question at Philburn.

"Who are those men?"

"Baseball players, sir," Philburn said. "We trounced them twenty-three to nothing."

"Baseball players?" Sherman said.

The baseball players went for the cadets. They charged, a drunken, ugly mob.

That act apparently bred courage in the Tilden men, and they rushed the dais, two hundred or more of them, pushing their way through the crowd, flinging eggs, tomatoes, rocks, a barrage of missiles.

On the dais, two men grabbed President Hayes and hustled him away. Sherman followed them. General Schofield and Colonel Bierce went the other way. Philburn and I stood, and then I headed across the dais toward the trees where Louise was with the children. But by the time I got there, she was gone, as were all the other women who had been sitting with her. I saw their party, tripping up the hill toward Schofield's house. They were safe.

I slipped back down the hill, into the cadet ranks. There I found a cadet colonel, and I grabbed his arm.

"Organize your command, sir!" I shouted at him. "Help me form a semicircle in front of this dais."

"Sir, yes, sir!" the young man responded. Then, turning to the corps: "First Regiment, form on me!"

Philburn came down beside me. "What are we to do?" he asked.

I grinned at him. "We fight, sir," I said. "Help me pull some of these boards loose."

And he and I began to dismantle the dais. Under the bunting, the boards were rough planks, some of them twelve feet in length. They made a cracking sound when Philburn and I pulled them loose.

"Keep pulling," I said to Philburn. Then I turned to the cadet colonel. I grabbed his shoulder and shouted in his ear, "Use these planks as weapons. Disperse them to your men."

"Sir, yes, sir!"

Then I moved out into the cadet corps, my sword drawn. "Back, boys, move back. Form a semicircle in front of the dais. Move back, boys."

I kept moving through the cadets, repeating my orders, holding my sword point up.

I saw another cadet officer. I accosted him. "Sir, move

your men back to the dais. We are forming a semicircle. You take the left flank. Tell the cadet colonel back there to take the right."

He was a yellow-haired boy, his eyes dancing with excitement.

"Yes, sir," he said. "This way, men!" he shouted to the cadets about him. "Follow me!"

Then I was in the thick of it.

The hairy mob was moving like an avalanche through the cadets, but the cadets were fighting back, their fists flying.

"Cadets, fall back!" I yelled, swinging my sword, trying to hit only with the flat side. I caught one fellow full on the side of his head and sent him reeling. Another swung an ax handle at me, which I parried with the sword, then backhanded him across the cheek, drawing blood.

"Back, boys!" I continued to command. "Back to the dais. Form up! Form up!"

I caught a rock then, square on my chest. It stunned me, but I didn't fall. Instead, I began wildly to swing the sword. My attackers didn't know it wasn't sharpened, and they held back.

"Pick up the fallen, men!" I yelled. "Pull them back to the dais!"

The cadets and I began to fall back then, slowly, just keeping the Yonkers hooligans at bay.

Then we were at the dais. Four hundred, a semicircle in

front of the dais, five and six men deep. Those in front had big, rough plank boards, which they used both to fend off missiles and to swing at the attackers.

On the left, the Tilden men were pushing hard. Some had sticks, nearly all had rocks and vegetables, which they flung with abandon.

I stood with Philburn in the midst of our defensive formation, and I told the cadets nearest me, "Gather the stones, boys! Return fire!"

Philburn had cadets helping him pry loose more boards. Sweat ran in rivulets off his face. When the boards were free, they were passed, hand over hand, to the front.

There were yells and grunts and more yells and more grunts. The battle was approaching a climax, I could tell. The Yonkers men and the Tilden men summoning up for one grand charge.

Then I heard Philburn, his voice rough and splendid.

"Men of West Point! Hold your line! Duty! Honor! Country!"

And there was a great cheer among the cadets, a resounding "Hurrah!"

Then a roar and the rattle of canister shot whistling through the air.

That cannon blast quieted everybody.

I turned to my right, and there, on a hill not fifty yards away, was General Schofield. He was standing next to a twelve-pound Napoleon that Colonel Bierce and three cadets were reloading. Smoke from the discharge wafted slowly about the group.

"Cadets!" Schofield said in a voice loud with command. "Remove yourselves from the line of fire. You civilians, put your hands up in the air and do not move."

The Napoleon was reloaded. I'd seen the load, canister shot. Schofield had directed the first load over the heads of the crowd, the grape whistling off into the distant river below. But this load was pointed downward, directly at the crowd. Colonel Bierce stood at the back of the cannon, a lighted puck in his hand.

Schofield stood, erect and imposing.

"Major Philburn," Schofield called. "Lead the cadets in this direction. They will form to my left."

Philburn worked his way through the mass, and the cadets began to form up to follow him. I stood, waiting to see what would happen next.

As the cadets moved out, Schofield spoke to the few hundred men left in the quad, all of whom stood with their hands in the air.

"Sit, gentlemen, where you are. Sit." Schofield's voice was as sharp and icy as a sliver. "If you try to run, I will give the order to fire. At this distance, we will kill half of you."

In the quad, the men began to sit.

I followed the last cadet up the hill.

———

Two cadets watched Darien and Cynthia Marie, one holding the little girl, who was asleep, the other bouncing Darien on his knee. Louise moved with Mrs. Schofield and other ladies through the remaining cadets, wiping at wounds, applying bandages. It was late afternoon and the hooligans had been dispersed. Only a few had actually been arrested. The corps was spread out on the grassy hillside, all of them sitting or lying in small groups, caught up in animated conversation.

Philburn and I stood down on the dilapidated dais. We'd overseen the removal of the Tilden men and the Yonkers baseball players and fans. The quad was now empty, littered with debris.

"It's around here somewhere," Philburn was saying, crouching and looking. "I don't remember who was holding it."

Up by the Napoleon, General Schofield was talking with General Sherman. They were a contrast in looks, Sherman thin and wiry, Schofield plump and solid. Sherman was smoking a cigar. Colonel Bierce stood slightly apart from the two generals.

"There it is," Philburn said, looking down. He was peering into a crack between two floorboards. "I'll get it."

And he walked the length of the dais, then down and around behind it.

I stood alone at the lectern, splattered with eggshell and tomato stains.

I'd give no speech today. The gods had spared me. I

heard Philburn rattling around beneath the dais. I looked out upon the empty quad. I felt a strange calm, a happiness even. This day, which was to have been my day, was almost over. All the ceremony had been lost, drained away by the actions of a drunken mob. And here I stood, a hero of riot. It brought a smile to my face.

"Here you go, Crofton."

Philburn was walking up the incline of the dais, a black, velvet-covered case in his hand.

He offered it to me. I took it.

"Open it," Philburn said.

Inside was the Victoria Cross, a blue-and-white ribbon circling it in its inset.

"I'm really sorry, Crofton," Philburn said. "Things turning out like they did."

I looked at him and smiled. "It was a fine day," I said.

I pushed the velvet-covered case inside my tunic, then walked down the dais, toward the hillside and my wife and children. I took the sleeping Cynthia Marie from the cadet holding her, then took Darien's hand.

I looked down at my sleeping daughter, her tiny face serene and beautiful. Then I looked for her mother, and saw Louise, bending over a cadet, wiping his forehead with a rag. She stood up and looked at me.

There, in the dappled shade, the sunlight dancing about her, she smiled at me.